CLAIMED BY THE DRAKARN WARRIOR LORD

DRAKARN MATES
BOOK 1

KATE RUDOLPH

ABOUT THE BOOK

I am a Drakarn warrior, protector of my people, master of blade and sky. Battles and threats are known to me, but *she* is a new mystery.

Terra storms into my world, unlike any female I've encountered. Smooth-skinned, wingless, claw-less... yet she radiates a fierce strength that ignites a firestorm within me.

Her defiance only fuels my desire. Her scent is my obsession, her touch a torment I crave.

Every instinct within me screams *mate*.

She's stubborn, resisting the bond that pulls us together, a bond she doesn't yet understand. But when a Drakarn finds his mate, he does not let go.

Terra harbors secrets, shadows that threaten the

fragile trust blooming between us. And when those secrets draw danger to her, I will unleash the inferno.

She is mine.

My heart. My soul.

I will scorch the skies and obliterate anyone who dares to harm who I cherish above all.

Darrokar

A soundless roar rumbled in the marrow of my bones.

I stood under the endless blood-red sky of Volcaryth, our twin suns glaring down like molten eyes. Above me, the heavens tore apart.

A vessel not of this world hurtled downward, a silvery behemoth engulfed in flames and blackened smoke. It screeched through the fiery clouds, splitting the horizon until it struck the molten surface of a distant lava lake. The impact sent shockwaves rippling across the landscape, the ground beneath my feet trembling with the screams of the dying heavens.

Lava erupted in great, fiery arcs, showering the

area in droplets of liquid fire that hissed and sizzled against the scorched earth.

Then, through the smoke and chaos, *she* appeared.

She staggered from the wreckage. Her form was framed by twisting pillars of flame, long hair cascading like molten copper caught in a breeze I couldn't feel. Her eyes—striking emerald, impossibly vibrant against her soot-streaked skin—locked onto mine as though she could see me, despite the vast distance between us. It was impossible. And undeniable.

And her scent ...

Gods above and below, her scent.

It was unlike anything I'd ever known, unlike the cloying sweetness of the forge or the sharp tang of battle. It was warm and intoxicating, like the first breath of air after emerging from the river's icy depths.

It filled my lungs and settled deep in my chest, igniting some part of me I'd never known before. My fangs burned, sharp twinges sparking along my gums. My tongue ... it ached, hypersensitive, as though begging to taste her, to confirm what my senses already screamed at me.

Mine.

Though she was an otherworldly figure surrounded by destruction, my every instinct roared with certainty. This stranger drenched in firelight and shadow belonged to me, and I ...

I belonged to her.

The sureness was maddening.

I wanted her, not with the fleeting yearning of warrior lust but with something infinitely deeper, something that clawed at the core of my being. My claws flexed involuntarily, tips scraping against the rocky surface beneath my feet.

"Who are you?" The question tore from my lips though she was too far away to hear.

She looked at me as though she'd heard the words, understood them—felt them. Her lips parted, and though I could hear no sound, her voice resonated in my very blood. A single word formed in her breath—just one. I couldn't make it out, but it vibrated through me, carving itself deep into my soul.

She raised her hand, pale against the encroaching flames, and reached toward me. My wings instinctively flared, as though they could bridge the impossible distance.

Mine.

The word burned through my mind again, sharpening as the air around me wavered, turning unbearably hot, even for someone born of fire and heat. My scales—hardened and scarred from countless battles—tingled unbearably, as though anticipating her touch, her claim. My battle-worn body, carved and unyielding, ached for her in a way that made no sense.

This was no battle. This was no war. And yet I felt as though I'd fought for lifetimes, bled and burned, just for this moment.

For her.

The dream shifted.

She was closer now. Her scent crushed me, heady and overwhelming, setting every nerve in my body aflame. Her fingertips brushed against my chest, tracing the deepest of my scars with an intimacy that made me growl. Her touch was firm.

Possessive.

My head dipped, her breath mingled with mine, and all I craved was—

Light. Blinding, burning light.

No, pain—searing, unbearable pain lancing through my fangs, my claws, my tongue—all the parts of me born to claim and devour. I snarled as the dream unraveled, her form dissolving before I could catch her, and then, abruptly, the world tilted, and I was falling.

Falling into shadows. Into silence. Into ...

My eyes snapped open with a sharp inhale, the echo of her touch still sizzling beneath my skin.

The glow of the heat crystals embedded in my chamber walls did little to stave off the pounding in my chest. My breaths came ragged, uneven. I shot upright, my claws gripping at the carved edges of the obsidian slab I called a sleeping platform. I stared down at my hands, the tremors running through them utterly foreign to me.

Darrokar, Warrior Lord of Scalvaris, did not shake.

But my fangs burned.

Closing my mouth did little to soothe the fiery ache in my jaw. I flexed my tongue, wincing as the faintest motion sent unbearable hypersensitivity ricocheting across my senses. My wings, half-unfurled, curled protectively around me.

Damned dreams.

I growled low, the sound vibrating through my chest, but it put no distance between me and the sensations clawing at me. The tingling along my claws, the phantom press of her fingers over my skin, the maddening scent that lingered in the air, entwining with the faint freshness of the river below.

I couldn't dismiss it—not as a trick of the mind,

not as a warrior's exhaustion or the effects of a poor night's rest. This was something deeper. I'd known of the fated bond only through stories and ritual, through the words of others. I'd never dreamed of it for myself.

And yet. She was real. *Somewhere*, she was real.

I rose from the slab, dragging my claws over its cool surface as though that might cure the chaos within me. It didn't help. My clawed feet touched the smooth volcanic rock of the chamber floor, and my wings drew close to my body, their membranes taut with tension.

Moving toward the sky tunnel carved into the ceiling, I narrowed my eyes to the faint stream of light streaking down from the twin suns. It was dim now. The sun shafts would soon burn brighter, but for now, this slice of sky was cool enough for reflection.

Reflection. The word felt weak, and the fire ravaging my senses left no room for hesitation.

I braced my hands against the angular edges of the tunnel's opening, letting the external heat press against my scales. My claws scraped at the volcanic stone, seeking some purchase, but there was no escaping the torrent within. It gnawed at me, simmering low in my gut and coiling tighter with every moment. I wanted to howl into the void, to demand the gods of my ancestors explain this madness.

Instead, I tilted my head back toward the narrow view of the heavens. Somewhere, far above this labyrinth of obsidian halls and warrior chambers, was the source of my agony—and my salvation. The dream ... it hadn't been my imagination. It was a call.

I didn't understand how or why. Or how to answer it.

It didn't matter.

I would find her. I would tear through realms known and unknown if that's what it took. Just as the scar across my chest was earned and worn with pride, I would bleed for this bond. I bared my teeth in a wild grin.

Whatever gods had decided this woman was mine had better prepare for what they'd unleashed.

My fangs ached again, sharper this time. My claws flexed, and the scent of her ghosted through my senses once more, dragging foreign sweetness through the heat of Volcaryth. My mate waited ... somewhere.

"Mine," I murmured to the silence of my chamber, the word taking an unfamiliar softness atop the granite edges of my voice.

ONE

DARROKAR

The ancient stories spoke of beings from far away worlds. That dream hanging heavy over my thoughts put those stories at the forefront of my mind.

But it was the dark streaks of smoke in the sky that showed me something truly otherworldly had come to visit.

The crash was a speck on the horizon, smoke curling upward to stain the crimson of Volcaryth's sky. The suns hung heavy above, their fiery rays bearing down on us in judgement. I led the flight, my wings carving smooth arcs through the scalding air. Behind me, the shadows of my warriors mirrored me —loyal, deadly, unshakable.

"The wreckage reeks of foreign metal," Rath

growled, his ruby-red scales catching a glint of light. "We should scour it clean before it festers."

I shot him a look over my shoulder. "Have you forgotten the difference between fear and reward?" My words cut sharp, a blade honed by years of command. "We don't eliminate the unknown until we understand it."

Rath huffed but said no more. He knew better than to push me, though the way the veins along his neck pulsed betrayed his simmering impatience. It was his strength and his flaw—an explosive temper that mirrored his namesake, a heart of flame forever on the verge of inferno.

Vyne glided closer to my left flank. His deep purple scales shimmered faintly in the glare of the suns, his voice as steady as the flow of the sacred river. "Whatever fell from the sky wasn't designed for Volcaryth. It can't endure this heat. Whatever, or whoever, survived that crash might need aid." His gaze flicked toward Rath. "We should at least assess before we destroy."

"Romantics and fools," Rath muttered, just loud enough for Vyne to hear. Vyne ignored it, his focus locked on the blackened trail of destruction ahead.

My vision narrowed as we drew closer, the chaotic

debris field growing more distinct. Twisted shards of unfamiliar metal jutted at jagged angles from the scorched earth, smoke curling like gnarled claws over the broken landscape. Steam geysers erupted sporadically around the crash site, their lethal hiss lending a sense of unease to the already chaotic scene. And amid it all—movement. Subtle, cautious, but definitely there.

"Scatter formation," I commanded. "Sweep the perimeter. Observe, but do not engage."

They obeyed without question, each veering off with practiced precision. Seeing them move as extensions of my will stoked my pride, though it was short-lived as I descended toward the heart of the wreckage. My instincts roared in my ears—both the calculated reasoning of a seasoned leader and the maddening pulse of something far older than violence or strategy.

Her.

The scent struck me like a blade to the chest, ripping through the stale heat of molten metal and burned earth. Sweet, rich, and intoxicating, it cut through everything to brand itself into my senses.

My wings stuttered mid-beat, and I barely corrected in time to avoid a graceless landing. My claws hit the rock with more force than I intended, the impact jarring up my legs and grounding me for the moment.

Where was she?

My fangs burned, an insistent throb that radiated straight to the base of my skull, and my tongue scraped against the roof of my mouth, extra sensitive in anticipation of the taste of her. A growl bubbled at the back of my throat, low and possessive. I forced it back, barely. This was no time for instinct to override reason—though I felt the tenuous grip I had on my control fraying with every breath.

Movement to my right. I snapped my head toward it, wings flaring wide in an automatic show of dominance. The motion was fleeting, barely a flicker —a shadow disappearing behind a jagged chunk of the fallen craft. But it was enough. My claws flexed against the scorched ground.

I advanced slowly, my frame tight and ready. This wasn't the erratic shift of lesser wildlife fleeing the chaos—it was calculated. Intelligent. And if the foreign scent mingling with hers was any indication, I wouldn't face her alone.

The first attack came swift and silent—a jagged hunk of metal hurtling toward me, spinning wildly like an improvised blade. I sidestepped easily, pivoting as it clanged against the stone behind me.

My lips curled into a savage grin. Stealth had its merits, but it could only take you so far against a Drakarn warrior.

Another projectile, this time from my left. I ducked, twisting my wings to shield my vulnerable flank as the air hummed with its passing. Rath and Vyne were watching now; I felt their shadows circling above, waiting to see how I handled the ambush. I gave no order, not yet. This was my moment to assess, to understand the enemy before deciding its fate.

A hiss tore through the air as a figure emerged—a woman, fierce and unrelenting, holding what looked like a metal staff stripped from the wreckage. Her hair, a cascade of molten red, caught the light, turning her into a living flame. Scars of soot streaked across her skin, evidence of her battle to survive the crash. Despite her apparent injuries, her stance was solid, her resolve unwavering.

She had no claws. No wings. No scales. Nothing but fragile skin and a tight-fitting, torn outfit made of some dark material that had to be soaking up the heat of the day.

Her eyes—emeralds sharper than any dagger—fixed on me like a predator assessing its prey.

I froze.

It was her.

A moment stretched into eternity as our gazes locked, the world shrinking until it contained only her. The scent of her overwhelmed me. My fangs pulsed in time with my thundering heartbeat. My wings flared wider unconsciously, a declaration I couldn't suppress.

She was magnificent.

And she was terrified.

Her grip tightened on the staff, and I recognized the emotion in her eyes—it was defiance, strength honed under unimaginable duress. She would fight, not because she believed she could win but because the act itself was all she had, a refusal to yield.

Behind her, a second woman emerged, slighter but no less fierce. Her makeshift weapon mirrored her companion's, though her stance was more defensive, her weight shifting subtly as she kept a wary eye on the skies.

"I'll give you one chance to stand down." My voice cut through the oppressive heat. I shifted my weight forward, claws digging into the rock, my intent clear. "You are not in a position to threaten, let alone win."

The copper-haired woman snarled—an admirable mimicry of an actual predator. She spoke then, her voice sharp and foreign, the language unfamiliar and edged with desperation. I didn't understand the words, but the meaning was clear enough: she would not surrender.

Beside me, Rath landed with a heavy thud, his laugh booming. "They don't even have claws, Darrokar. Let me handle this," he said, hefting his lavaforged blade as though the mere act of drawing it ended all debates. "Two strikes, and they'll scatter like ash."

"No," I growled, the single word laced with steel. My gaze never left her, the connection between us tightening like a noose. "She's mine."

Rath froze, startled into silence by the force of my claim. Good. He didn't need to understand the depths of it, not now. Recognition burned through me, raw and undeniable. I would not allow anyone else to interfere in what was written into my very bones.

She stepped forward, her courage foolish yet compelling, and the impossibility of it all struck me anew. How could someone so fragile stand her ground against creatures born of fire and war? How could she stir something within me I'd long thought missing?

But she did, and I was powerless against it.

"Mine," I murmured again, the word barely audible but thrumming with intent.

And she flinched. Not visibly—not to anyone who wasn't watching her as closely as I was—but I felt it. A flicker of something in her challenging gaze.

Recognition? Fear?

Impossible. The distance between our worlds was greater than the void of stars she must have crossed to fall here.

Yet ... she knew me.

I was certain of it.

I stepped closer, ignoring the warning hiss of her blade scraping against the stone. The air between us crackled, alive with tension. The heat of Volcaryth paled in comparison to the fire she ignited within me. Still, I curved my claws inward, forced my wings to lower slightly. Despite everything, I didn't want to frighten her more than I already had.

"Who. Are. You?" I demanded, my voice a low rumble that trembled with the weight of a thousand battles fought and won. This was a different kind of war—one I wasn't sure even I could win.

Even as her staff rose in defiance and her companion shouted something unintelligible, I prayed she wasn't an enemy I'd have to put down.

Because killing her would destroy me.

TWO

TERRA

This was bad. Really bad.

Worse than any of us could have imagined.

The feral roar of the alien's voice rumbled through the air just as Vega ducked a perfectly timed swing of a serrated, glowing blade. I could barely hear myself think over the clanging of makeshift weapons and the reverberation of Vega's curses alongside Kira's sharp orders.

Every fiber of my body told me to keep fighting—to plant my boots firmly in this hellscape of molten debris and give everything I had to protect the others. And yet ...

I couldn't.

Not because my body felt weak—it didn't.

Despite our ship's crash and the oppressive heat and the boiling haze of this hell planet threatening to pull me under, I had strength left in my hands, surging through my muscles like a coiled snake ready to strike.

But when the alien male stalked toward me, his massive wings flaring wide like a predator closing in on cornered prey, I hesitated.

My chest burned as though something fiery and alive had been ignited beneath my ribs. My mouth felt as dry as this red desert while, weirdly, watering at the same time, a sensation that left a metallic tang on the back of my tongue.

And then, there was the scent.

Hot, sharp, masculine—it seared through the chaos, cutting through the smoke and sweat. It should have terrified me, should have sent me scrambling backward in retreat. Instead, every nerve in my body tightened in reckless, traitorous awareness, dragging me forward toward *him*.

This wasn't just a *what the hell is going on* moment. This was an entire *what the hell is wrong with me*.

"Terra, move!" Vega's sharp voice yanked me back to reality. My head whipped around just in time to see her block a blow with what was left of a metallic railing, the impact sending sparks skittering across the heated stone.

Adrenaline surged.

"Vega, fall back!" I barked, my voice hoarse but steady, even as my gaze slid traitorously back toward him.

He wasn't just watching me—I could swear he was freaking *claiming* me with just his eyes.

Golden irises pinned me in place, holding me as solidly as if his claws had already locked around my neck. The intensity there didn't match the mess of the scene around us. This was something else entirely.

Something wild.

A flash of movement had me pivoting, avoiding a sidelong blow. Another alien, large but leaner than mine—no, not *mine*, what the hell—angled in my direction with his blade raised. His scales shimmered faintly with the planet's fiery light, but I barely had time to register his features beyond the immediate recognition of him not being *him*.

Hawk's sharp whistle drew his attention just long enough for me to swivel behind him, a desperate swing of my improvised weapon enough to knock his blade off course. The ground beneath us groaned, steam rising in violent hisses as nearby geysers threatened another eruption.

"Terra!" Kira shouted, her panic-tinged voice cutting through the haze. "We're outnumbered! Selene and Lexa have the civilians covered, but if we don't—"

I cut her off with a harsh gesture because I already knew her point deep inside, the same way I recognized no number of clever maneuvers were going to help us now.

We'd drawn our line in the sand, but this hell planet's blistering winds had long since erased it.

"Stand down!" I ordered, my voice firm, clearer than I felt inside. My gaze swung to Vega next, who was already cornered closer to where Hawk tried to angle yet another hurl of debris. "*Stand. Down.*"

The reluctance in Vega's eyes mirrored my own internal struggle, but she nodded stiffly before stepping closer. As the others abandoned their positions one by one, scrambling for what little cover the terrain allowed, the shame of surrender twisted through me like jagged glass.

I *hated* this. Hated every fiber of my body for even considering it. And yet ...

Some part of me was oddly at peace with the decision, if only to prevent more harm.

I dropped my weapon and raised my hands, slow and deliberate, forcing myself not to meet the infernal heat of his gaze as he approached. Before I could speak—or gesture more clearly—he rumbled something low in his impossibly deep voice.

The sound carved its way through every level of my being, sinking into places I didn't know existed.

A wild flush rose to my throat before spreading upward, the betrayal of my own reaction coloring my complexion as my knees hit the ground.

The scorch-pain that had radiated dully in my chest spiked.

Then, he touched me.

It was a grip—not gentle but restrained power, claws not bared, hand unyielding but careful. His warmth enveloped me even through those reinforced tactical fibers of my cryo gear.

Except warmth was wrong. Wrong and far from describing the molten flush centered just below my ribcage.

The growl he gave then—alien threats or promises—I didn't know nor care which. Everything about those tonal complexities was vivid and sent heat straight to my core.

I had to be going crazy.

His voice was a brand, searing itself onto me. I couldn't understand the word he spoke, but its intention carried through the air like heat off the lava banks. It resonated with something primordial in me, silencing even the rippling hiss of geysers and shouts of my people.

I swallowed hard, my mouth watering in a way that was distinctly unnatural given the situation. His scent—the fiery, predatory warmth of it—fanned the flames of my confusion, nudging my focus away from my team's safety toward something far more personal, far more dangerous.

The alien squatted lower, his physicality looming over me like something I could feel. Those golden eyes, their slitted vertical irises narrowing slightly as though in calculation, locked onto my face.

"Stop," I bit out, my voice cracking but firm. Around us, the sounds of Vega growling her defiance and Hawk and Kira shifting to regroup were a distant murmur, as if the two suns above had dipped closer and drawn the alien and me into our own private storm.

He tilted his head at my outburst, his wings shifting behind him in a cascade of webbed black and faint sparks of glowing orange veins, like magma running beneath the surface. It should have been the stuff of nightmares, a predator crouched above me without the barest hint of human softness.

Instead, the burn within my chest pulsed, an undeniable urge to lean closer to him—which was precisely why I grit my teeth and tightened every muscle in defiance.

"I said *stop!*" I barked again, emphasizing the words with a shove against his hand where it gripped my arm. It didn't move; his strength was absolute. He could have crushed the bone beneath his hold, but I could feel the control.

Instead of retreating, I met his gaze with every ounce of fury and confusion swirling inside of me, forcing the trembling of my fingers to still.

He murmured something again, softer this time, as though coaxing a wild animal out of hiding. There were no harsh consonants in his alien tongue, just a series of low, rolling syllables that wrapped around my senses like a smoldering caress.

And then—oh god, *then*—his claws brushed along the bare skin of my wrist, light enough to skirt the surface but heavy enough to light up every nerve beneath it.

Heat rippled down my spine, a supernova of sensation erupting unseen between us. My lips parted in a quick inhale, the air thick with heat, sweat, and *him*. My body betrayed me again, shifting forward as though drawn, even as my brain screamed at me to *pull away, now, before it's too late.*

"Get your hands off her!" Vega's voice shattered the narrowing fog, sharp as shattered glass and laced with rage. My head snapped toward her in time to see her jerking a metal shard upward, but she was too close to one of the other warriors—a scarlet-scaled beast whose fangs bared at the threat.

"No! No, wait—stand *down*! I've got this!" My voice tore out of me again, this time larger than just the alien and me. It broke Vega's motion with a half-second pause, long enough that when the blade-armored tip of my assailant's *tail* flicked toward her, the alien didn't run her through.

The alien never took his eyes off me. His golden stare narrowed slightly, the predator in him assessing *me*—not for my fragile position on my knees, not as prey, but as something else.

Something I was scared to examine too deeply.

I didn't know what I expected—some grand gesture of violence, a moment where he would crush me beneath his power and leave no doubt about where his people and mine stood in this bizarre standoff.

Instead, his grip softened even more, claws grazing my skin in a way that felt uncomfortably ... intimate. It was as though he had heard the unspoken plea for control in my voice and answered with a show of restraint so deliberate it made my breath hitch.

His mouth moved again, the alien syllables wrapping around each other like molten metal. I couldn't make sense of the words, but something burned through the language barrier, something deeper than intent. It wasn't just *what* he said—it was *how*. The way it traveled through the humid air between us and curled itself into my subconscious.

I tried to yank my arm back, but his fingers tightened just enough to hold me still. His scent hit me again, wild and fiery, dragging my attention back to him.

"You don't understand what surrender means, do you?" I hissed, my voice low enough for only him to hear. Anger laced my words, but it wasn't the pure fury I'd leaned on for survival before. This was too tangled—too infused with something else to be simple rage.

His slitted gaze flicked over my face, calculating. He tilted his head to the side, lips pulling into something that wasn't quite a snarl but wasn't entirely neutral either. The motion distracted me for one dangerous second, enough for Vega's voice to cut through the heated haze between us.

"Terra, let me fucking fight!" she snapped, her ragged breath giving away how close to the edge her own reserves were. I could feel her tension radiating even as Hawk moved in beside her, both of them too battered and too smart not to know the inevitable conclusion if this dragged out.

But I couldn't let their lives end here.

"Stop it," I said again, louder this time, feeling the weight of every word grind against the raw edges of my pride. My jaw clenched as I spoke, as though physically forcing the surrender from my throat. "All of you. Now."

Hawk, Kira, and Vega hesitated, unsure, searching my expression for answers. And why wouldn't they? I hadn't exactly briefed them on "kneeling in front of fiery alien dragon men" as part of our survival strategy. But they *had* been in enough impossible situations with me to recognize that this wasn't a bluff—they just didn't have to like it.

The alien male made a deep sound in the back of his throat, almost a purr, as his gaze lingered on my face. It wasn't a kind sound—not quite mocking, but close. As though he saw that moment—my humility, my defiance, and my desperation—and enjoyed how it tasted.

"What?" I snapped at him, my own patience wearing thin under the weight of his attention. "You think this is funny?"

His response was to move even closer. I barely registered the shift before I felt the heat of his breath on my cheek. His other hand, the one not firmly locked around my arm, hovered near my face for the briefest of moments before withdrawing again.

The sharp tang of his scent—the alien fire and molten embers—deepened, igniting that physical insanity that had taken root inside me. The pulse beneath my ribs burned hotter. My teeth and tongue ached again, and for one horrifying second, I jerked my lips shut as though that would keep whatever was happening to me at bay.

His rumble deepened, the vibration crawling into my chest and settling there like an inferno. He wasn't laughing. There was no mockery there, not really. What I heard in that sound—what I *felt* in it— was darker.

Hungrier.

And I hated that some part of me was hungry too.

"Terra," Hawk called again, the concern in her

voice sharpening. She wasn't used to seeing me like this—none of them were. And why would they be? Leadership, decisiveness, composure—that was what they knew of me. That was who I *was*. I didn't lose myself. Not in combat, not in isolation, not even kneeling on a battlefield under dual alien suns while some hulking predator branded my soul with his gaze.

Except right now, I wasn't sure that was entirely true.

The alien tilted his head, considering me—or maybe simply savoring whatever curse-bound connection had glued me to him. His wings fanned wide with a slow, deliberate stretch that made their sheer size unavoidable. In any other context, I might have called them magnificent, the veins glowing faintly in the hell planet's heat. But all I could focus on was the fact that his body had shifted to block me further from the others.

Possession.

The thought made me shiver in a way I hated. Not just because it felt accurate, but because it didn't feel entirely unwelcome—and that terrified me.

As though sensing the shift in my thoughts, his claws flexed lightly around my arm, a silent acknowledgment that sent another unwelcome flush of heat coursing through my body. I yanked harder this time, pulling back with everything I had, but his grip didn't waver. It didn't tighten, either.

He rumbled something else, those alien words rumbling in his chest more than his throat, and leaned just a fraction closer. This time, his scent overwhelmed me completely, leaving no room for coherent thoughts beyond my own confused, traitorous reactions.

"I don't know what you want," I hissed, my voice sharp but uneven thanks to the inexplicable sensation building inside me. "But I'll make this real simple: The others? They're not part of this. You deal with me and *only* me."

Behind me, I could hear my team shifting uneasily. I didn't dare try to meet their gazes, not when I couldn't guarantee the calm façade I always wore would hold. Letting them see would be worse than whatever these creatures decided to do with us.

The alien didn't move at first. His eyes burned into me, searching, weighing something I couldn't see. Words slipped through his lips again—low, deliberate, foreign—and his claws eased, if only just.

Then, without warning, he pulled me closer. Not roughly, but with the kind of demand that left no room for negotiation. His presence dwarfed mine, even without the physical reality of his size towering over me.

And then, he spoke the first word I understood—not from language, but from the resonance in my very bones.

"*Luvae.*"

Mine.

Vega cursed every step of the way for the first mile or so. If she had slightly less discipline, she might have made a run for it. But we had six women hiding in a hidden cave not far from the crash site.

We might have been captured, but they were still free. I wasn't sure that would actually be any help. Most of them were civilians, and they'd rip through supplies fast.

Figuring out what this planet was, who these aliens were, had to be the top priority.

Was there even the slightest chance of sending out a distress signal? How far were we from Earth? I had so many questions and no hope for answers. Not now.

The aliens marched us through the hot sand to a barely seen cave entrance and led us down beneath the surface, past twisting tunnels and rushing rivers that carved their way through walls of volcanic rock.

I breathed in thankful gulps of the underground air. It wasn't cool, not really, but the moisture and the shade made it feel like paradise.

The scale of it was overwhelming at first—colossal stone archways leading to cavernous halls that thrummed with life. The sharp, rhythmic clang of weapons echoed in the background, accompanied by commanding voices in the alien tongue. Even beneath their guarded stares, I found myself wanting to look at it all, to memorize every detail.

For survival, I told myself. But part of me couldn't help but feel a connection to the raw power of this place.

And now, we were there. Trapped. Hard, uneven stone underfoot, cool despite the heat of the planet. A single, heavy metal door secured us within. No windows. No clear way out. Alone with my team and too many unanswered questions.

Hawk paced a short distance near the far wall, keeping her eyes sharp on the door. Kira was crouched next to her pack, which she'd tucked behind what little cover the room provided, her fingers deft as she rummaged through it. Vega sat with her back to a wall, legs folded under her, her expression sharp and calculating.

She was studying everything, cataloging it like she always did. And me? I stood quietly near the door, rubbing at the faint ache on my arm where that alien had grabbed me. No bruising. No break in the skin. Yet I could still feel the heat of his claws there, like a brand.

Or maybe it was his presence that left that mark.

I was ashamed of how vivid the memory was. His golden eyes had burned through me with an intensity I couldn't shake. That deep voice, unfamiliar but alive with meaning, haunted me. And worst of all was the word he said—or more accurately, the way it felt.

That single syllable reverberated in my chest long after he'd pulled away.

Luvae.

I clenched my fists against the thought, forcing my feet to brace wide as if that would steady me entirely. My tongue connected briefly with the roof of my mouth, and I immediately regretted the action when that now-familiar tingling sensation kicked in again, traveling the length of my jaw like a warning. Or a threat.

God, I hated this.

Hawk's voice broke through the tense silence, sharp and practical, "What's the plan, Captain?"

She always said "Captain" like that, as if I needed the reminder. Like she knew my mind was racing, that I needed the weight of authority to stop me from spiraling into personal doubts. And damn if she wasn't right. Again.

There was no need to remind her that we'd left our ranks behind back on Earth before climbing onto the generation ship. We'd all signed on to be security forces at the new colony when we woke up.

This place? Definitely not part of the plan.

I inhaled deeply, forcing myself to meet her gaze. "We need to take stock," I said, my voice steadier than I felt. "Assess resources. What do we have? What do we know?"

"Kira?" Vega prompted.

"Still got my pack," Kira confirmed, her voice low but colored with quiet triumph as she pulled out something small and black. "They didn't stop me from bringing it. Either they underestimated us, or they don't fully understand human tech."

There were aliens back on Earth, but none like this. The travelers who had made it to us had never hinted at a place like this. These aliens, these monsters reminded me of dragons in a way I couldn't quite explain, and I was worried we were about to become their hoard.

Or dinner.

"What's that?" Vega moved closer as Kira turned the device over in her hands, inspecting it.

"Basic translators," Kira said, offering a faint smile. "They're not perfect—more like a rough filter of language patterns—but they should let us listen in. With some quick tweaks, I might even get them working both ways, but it might take some time."

Vega was immediately wary. "We don't want them to know we can understand them. That gives away our only advantage. Better to keep it one-sided, use it to gather intel."

Kira frowned but didn't argue, her focus dropping back to the device in her hands. She knew Vega rarely argued unless she was absolutely certain she was right. She handed out the thin slips of metal and showed us how to attach them to the skin behind our ears where they'd be hidden by hair. Even if the aliens caught sight of them, they sort of looked like scars. They wouldn't know we could understand them.

"They're powered by bioelectricity," said Kira. "No need for a power source."

When the translator powered on, I heard a faint buzzing in my ear, and my head ached for a second before the pain faded.

"We need to figure out what they want from us," Vega said, leaning back against the wall again. "And then if escape becomes viable, we act."

"Escape?" Hawk crossed her arms. "In case you didn't notice, this place is built like an actual fortress. And even if we made it to the surface, this whole damn planet's trying to kill us."

"So?" Vega shot back sharply. Her gray eyes narrowed in the eerie glow, steel and fire beneath her calm, collected surface. "We've got people out there who have no idea what happened to us. Do you want to just leave them?"

"No," Hawk's tone was grim, "I'm suggesting we don't act out of desperation. Until we know what we're dealing with, laying low is the safer play."

"Enough," I said, raising my voice just enough to halt the back-and-forth. "Both of you are right." My gaze flicked between them, making sure they were listening. "We keep track of what options are on the table. If an opportunity presents itself, we take it. But until then, we stay alive by keeping our heads down, assessing the situation, and not drawing unnecessary attention."

Hawk's shoulders eased slightly, and Vega gave a begrudging nod. It wasn't perfect, but it would hold. For now.

Kira's voice, softer but no less certain, drew my attention next. "For what it's worth, I don't think they're going to kill us," she said. "If they wanted us dead, they had plenty of chances already."

None of us disagreed, though the unspoken doubt hung heavy in the air. Wanting something from us didn't mean we were safe. It just meant we weren't expendable. Yet.

The door groaned suddenly, massive and heavy as it swung inward. The sound reverberated through the room. My heart climbed straight to my throat, my senses sharpening as I braced for whatever entered next.

Him.

The heat I'd struggled to push down earlier rose again, coiling deep within me. His frame filled the entryway, larger-than-life and impossibly commanding.

Obsidian-black scales gleamed faintly in the

light, touched with crimson undertones that practically glowed. His wings took up the space around him like he owned it, folding close enough to brush the edges of his imposing shoulders. Behind him, three others followed in silence—two of them vaguely familiar from the crash site, though I barely spared them a glance.

No, my focus was locked entirely on him.

He stepped forward, steady and purposeful, and though the chamber wasn't small by any means, it immediately felt too tight. Like he was sucking all the air from the room with his presence alone.

My pulse quickened, my body tense and alert for reasons I couldn't fully explain. It was beyond just survival instincts now. This was something else.

His golden eyes found mine without hesitation. No scanning the room, no split-second hesitation. Just ... me. Always me.

I hated the way that softened edge of his gaze hit me, vibrating down to my bones. I clenched my fists at my sides and forced myself not to step back—to hold my ground despite the almost suffocating pull of whatever unnatural gravity seemed to bind him and me closer.

One word fell from his mouth, low and resonant.

"Come."

Even without the translator, the tone carried a layered command I felt as much as heard. There was no mistaking who he meant—even without the sharp, obvious shift of his golden stare boring into mine.

The others bristled immediately, their instincts screaming at them to protect me. Hawk rose to her feet fully, her jaw tight and her body stiff as a board. Vega stiffened, but wisely said nothing, though her dangerously calculating eyes flicked quickly toward me for a barely noticeable second. Kira tensed, balancing protectiveness with obscuring the translator still in her hands.

"You can't expect us to let her—"

I cut Hawk off with a sharp motion, tilting my head just slightly in warning. She quieted but didn't move, and I adjusted my focus back to the towering figure in the room. He hadn't spoken again yet, nor moved much closer, but the weight of his expectant presence left room for little else.

I didn't have the luxury to argue—not with them, not with *him*. It wasn't about surrender. It was about survival. Every choice I made had to balance the survival of the team against the unknown variables of what came next.

So I lifted my chin, squared my shoulders, and

forced every ounce of confidence into my voice when I spoke.

"Fine," I said, keeping it clipped, sharp, and neutral. "Just me." He couldn't understand me, I knew, but I pointed at my chest and hoped he got the idea.

He tilted his head slightly, those brilliant golden eyes narrowing just a fraction—and for a moment, I felt the weight of his scrutiny like a burning ember pressed against raw nerve endings. Then he simply inclined his head, an almost unnervingly deliberate acknowledgment.

"Captain, you don't have to—" Hawk started again, stepping forward.

"I do," I cut her off again, softer this time. I didn't look at her—not because I didn't care, but because meeting her eyes would only crack the carefully constructed weight of authority I was clinging to right now. "Stay with the others. Watch. Listen. And *wait*."

The last word was for all of them, though it hung heavier on Hawk's shoulders than mine. Her jaw tightened visibly, but she nodded ever so slightly. I knew her well enough to sense the storm she was holding back.

Drawing one deep, steadying breath, I stepped

toward the massive alien looming near the chamber's entrance. My legs were steady, though every instinct screamed at me to stop, to fight.

But I couldn't. Not yet.

His gaze burned over me, intense and searing as molten fire, as he turned and led me wordlessly out into the dim glow of the underground city.

FOUR

TERRA

The alien—my alien, I guess—said something quietly to the others. Despite my translator, I couldn't pick up on it. I just had to hope he wasn't telling them to do anything nasty towards my team.

If they got hurt, I'd never forgive myself.

I followed my alien through winding caverns that towered high overhead, high enough that some of the aliens were flying rather than walking.

The cavern was so high it was almost possible to forget we were in a cave.

We walked through a courtyard where aliens fought and drilled. It was strange that it was so bright even though we were underground. High above, there were breaks in the ceiling, allowing light in.

He led me to a building and opened a door. I

stepped into a room, my boots scraping lightly against the smooth stone floor as the door groaned shut behind me. The sound was final, a low, resonant thud that ricocheted through my chest.

I didn't flinch—wouldn't let myself—but it took effort. I breathed deep, but it didn't push out the taut, simmering unease curling under my ribs.

The first thing I noticed was the heat. Not stifling or oppressive like the planet's surface, but a different kind of warmth, radiating in waves as if the room pulsed with life. Crystals embedded in the walls glowed faintly, their golden and red hues shifting like flickering embers. They bathed everything in a soft, otherworldly glow, making the space feel both cavernous and intimate.

He stepped into my peripheral vision, and I held my ground. His movements were purposeful, a predator's grace that drew my eyes against my will. The leather-like material of the fitted armor over his dark scales caught the light, and my fingers ached to touch.

Stupid, traitorous fingers.

His wings shifted subtly, brushing the edges of the room as if claiming the space, and by extension, me.

Focus, Terra.

"Darrokar," he said, his voice a low rumble that commanded attention. He pointed at his chest, his sharp, clawed hand resting there for a beat before he locked his golden eyes on mine. I felt the gravity of his presence pull at me, like standing too close to the edge of a cliff.

Two could play that game. I straightened, a thin smile carving across my face—unflinching, even though my pulse pounded against my ribs. I pointed at myself. "Terra," I told him evenly, my voice steady despite the low hum of apprehension under my skin.

His head tilted, just slightly, as he studied me. The sharp contours of his face softened for a moment, some flicker of recognition crossing his features. It faded quickly, replaced by the same unreadable expression that had unsettled me earlier.

"Terra," he echoed, voice rolling over the syllables like thunder. The way he said it felt unfamiliar, yet *right*, and I actively tamped down the strange heat unfurling in my chest.

Pull it together, soldier.

Satisfied, he turned away and gestured toward the far side of the room, where steam drifted lazily from the surface of a massive stone tub set into the floor. Water—not molten rock or some alien equivalent—but clear, bubbling water filled it, the surface shimmering faintly in the light.

Tub was an understatement. It was basically a pool.

I stared at it, momentarily caught off guard. He wanted me to ... What, take a bath? After being marched across the desert, imprisoned, and dragged down here like a prisoner—or worse? He expected me to relax like it was some grand spa day?

"You've got to be fucking kidding me," I muttered. His eyebrows twitched, but his expression remained unchanged.

I'd be lying if I said a bath didn't sound amazing. I was covered in a week's worth of desert filth and who knew how many years of stale air from the cryo-sleep chamber. The stone bath looked like something out of a dream. But I had a feeling that every time I took something from the alien—from Darrokar—there'd be a price to pay.

He gestured again, this time more insistently, his clawed hand slicing through the air toward the tub before his gaze flicked back to me. I could feel the weight of the command, even if the words weren't there.

I narrowed my eyes, forcing myself to stay calm,

though the urge to snap rose hot and fast. My options were limited. If I flat-out refused, he might force me or worse. I didn't know what it would cost me—or my team—and I sure as hell wasn't about to start something I wasn't prepared to finish.

But.

He didn't get to just make me to do a striptease right in front of him. That wasn't how this worked. Survival didn't mean submission.

Independence intact, but acting dumb, I tilted my head and feigned ignorance, gesturing toward myself with exaggerated confusion as if to say: *What do you want from me?*

He clearly didn't buy it, the tightening of his jaw proved that much. Without breaking stride, he strode toward a chaise carved from obsidian and covered in silky pillows situated near the room's center and lowered himself onto it, every move calculated.

The tension in my muscles coiled tighter as I watched him recline, propping an arm on the back of the chaise as if this were a casual negotiation rather than ... whatever the hell it was. His golden eyes remained locked on me, unyielding, and damned if I didn't feel cornered in this vast room.

The door creaked open then, and two figures entered, slim and silent. They moved gracefully—

quiet servants who carried a large tray between them. They had wings but didn't have claws.

No, that wasn't it.

Their claws had been filed down to barely anything, and their hands looked almost like mine, if bonier. Was that something these aliens did to keep their servants from rebelling? Or was it their choice?

It wasn't like I could ask. And even if he could understand me, I doubted Darrokar would answer.

My stomach clenched sharply at the sight of food arranged in vivid, unfamiliar splashes of color. Fruits that shimmered like gemstones, steaming pieces of cooked meat glistening with glaze, and a pitcher of liquid that glittered faintly in the dim light. The smell, rich and inviting, hit me with an intensity I wasn't prepared for.

I hadn't realized how long it had been since I'd eaten properly until then. Rations from the crash site only went so far, and saving water was becoming a brutal necessity. My body screamed to lunge for the tray, but I froze when Darrokar shifted.

He made a harsh sound—commanding, territorial. His clawed hand extended outward, palm flat toward the food, before it gestured again toward the tub. The meaning didn't require translation.

Not until you bathe.

Seriously?

Anger burned hot in my chest and sharper than my hunger. My first instinct was to refuse outright, to make a stand then and there. But survival whispered caution. Picking a fight over food I couldn't secure for myself was a losing battle.

Watching him closely, I took a slow step forward, then another, my eyes flicking deliberately between him and the tray.

He didn't move, his expression impassive, but as soon as I stretched a hand toward what looked like a caramelized piece of meat, his clawed grip shot out lightning fast. Before I could react, my wrist was enclosed in heat and strength, dragged upward just enough to make me stumble closer to him.

"Wash yourself," he hissed, my translator having no problem at picking up his words.

My heartbeat spiked violently. I wanted to pull back on instinct, but his grip was firm, holding me steady as he rose in one smooth, fluid motion that had him towering over me again. The world narrowed alarmingly.

My brain scrambled to control the interaction, to tip the balance back to neutral ground, but Darrokar had other plans. Slowly, deliberately, his other hand rose to point once more at the steaming bath behind us, his command clear.

Fuck.

"Fine," I bit out, not caring that he wouldn't understand the sarcasm laced in my tone.

He'd get the message in my posture, in the way I refused to look away as I wrenched my wrist from his grip. My skin tingled where his claws had pressed—not hard enough to pierce, but firm enough to leave an impression that was more than just physical.

Heat burned in my veins now, distinct and unwelcome. A little too familiar.

I turned sharply on my heel and stalked toward the tub, determined to do this my way if I was doing it at all. Rebellion was futile in the grander sense, but there was power to be found in the smaller victories.

Without pausing, I stepped directly into the steaming water, my boots sinking into its depths with a faint splash that echoed in the silent room. The fabric of my pants clung to my skin, the sensation cloying and uncomfortable as I lowered myself fully into the bath, clothes and all.

When I leaned back against the edge, crossing my arms defensively over my chest, I finally let myself look his way. His expression was ... unexpected.

No anger. No disappointment.

Amusement flickered faintly at the edges of his golden gaze, and the sight of it made me press my teeth together in frustration.

Then he tilted his head back and laughed.

The sight of her, drenched and defiant in my bath, sent a blade of desire straight through me.

She didn't cower. She didn't plead. Instead, she faced me with those striking green eyes, her chin tilted in a warrior's challenge, shoulders squared as if daring me to push her further.

Water streamed from her soaked clothes, rippling around her, but she gave no sign of discomfort. She was magnificent—a contradiction of softness and steel, fragility and stubborn defiance.

I couldn't stop the grin before I let a low, rumbling laugh escape, filling the chamber with its echo. It wasn't a sound I often made, and it caught even me off guard. Her head tilted slightly at the sound, her eyes narrowing, but not before I caught a flicker of something—confusion? Surprise? Perhaps something deeper that she hadn't meant to show.

Desire warred with my warrior-strong self-control. Everything about her—her scent, her defiance, her very presence—tested my patience in ways nothing had before.

It wasn't just the mate-bond roaring beneath my skin, demanding I claim what was mine. She wove herself into my senses, made me hyper-aware of every breath, every subtle change in her expression.

This was a battle, but not one I could fight with claws or sword.

I turned away, stalking toward the massive window that overlooked my city, my back to her now. The pull she had on me was maddening, but I needed the distance to collect myself. My wings flexed as I drew a breath that seared hotter than molten rock, willing my control back into place.

Below us, Scalvaris sprawled out in all its harsh beauty. The rushing river snaked through the city, our lifeline and what made Scalvaris habitable. Great towers of obsidian rose high, their jagged spires glistening in the glow from the water and sky shafts that let in the light. Warriors trained in the combat pits, the sound of steel cutting through the air even faintly audible here.

I pointed out the window. "Scalvaris," I said firmly, the weight of the word sharp in the chamber. It fell heavy between us, and I stopped myself from glancing back at her, curious to see if she would recognize the significance of the gesture.

She'd shifted in the bath, her eyes now fixed on the scene beyond the window. Something shifted in her expression—curiosity, maybe even wonder—as her gaze swept over the city. I could tell she tried to suppress it, but the faint parting of her lips, the way her brow softened for just a moment, betrayed her. And then it was gone, neutral steel replacing it once more.

"Scalvaris," I repeated, louder now, drawing her attention away from the view. Her eyes darted to me, wary again as if she thought I might try something. I lifted an arm to gesture toward the city and held her gaze. When I spoke the word a third time, her eyes narrowed slightly, as if realizing my intent. And then, slowly, she attempted to repeat it.

It wasn't a perfect approximation. Her voice rounded the edges, softened the harsh crack of the "v" sound. But it was enough to make the mate-bond snap taut within me, the word sparking something dark and deep. It didn't matter how far she'd come, how different her people might be.

There she was, speaking *my* language, standing in *my* city. Nowhere in all the stars could fate weave something more potent.

I nodded slightly, encouraging her.

"Scalvaris," she said again, more force this time. My chest rumbled with satisfaction. The mate-bond burned brighter, tighter. My mate. My future. All I had to do now was convince her to accept what I already knew.

I crouched low beside the edge of the bath, close enough to feel the tension radiating from her body. That scent—wariness tinged with fear—hit me again, sharp and unwelcome. It was a knife pressed against my warrior's instincts, demanding I tread carefully when every fiber of my being told me to act. My claws scraped against the stone tiles beneath me, but I forced my hands to remain steady, curved inward to show that, for now, I meant no harm.

The bond howled within me, insistent and unrelenting. Soothe her, it demanded, shield her, claim her.

My instincts roared their agreement in a frenzy, but I smothered them the way I had hundreds of times in battle—as a leader, not a beast. This wasn't the moment for dominance or possession. Not yet.

Not until I could strip the fear from her gaze and replace it with something far more potent.

My eyes drifted to the tray of food one of the servants had brought earlier. Crystal fruit, redclaw meat, lava-crusted bread—sustenance meant for warriors, each piece glistening and steaming in its fresh preparation.

Her eyes darted to the meal, then back to me. I saw it then, flickering just beneath her defiance—a flash of carefully guarded hunger. She wanted it, needed it, though she wouldn't dare reach for it. Not yet. There was too much uncertainty between us, too much unknown.

And still, she watched me, her jaw tight, her battered resolve holding firm even as her body betrayed her needs.

Magnificent.

But my control was wearing thin. The weight of her closeness, her scent, and the heat of her presence soaked into me like magma against stone. She didn't yet understand who—or what—I was.

Without a word, I stood, shrugging off the leather armor with practiced ease. My tail curled behind me as the heat in the room licked at my exposed scales, every inch of me unrepentant and bare. I didn't look away from her as the last piece fell. Her wide eyes snapped to me. Lower, to the thick cords of muscles across my chest. Lower still as her gaze followed the long, scaled length of my tail ... the hilt of my cock beneath my abdomen.

Her attention lingered, her pupils dilating, and for a single beat, every shield in her expression fractured. Surprise. Curiosity. Something darker that made the mate-bond growl with triumph. And then she realized I was watching her. Her head jerked back up, her cheeks flushing a deeper shade. She threw her gaze back towards the city.

I let my wings unfurl slightly, the movement calm and deliberate as I stepped into the bath beside her, silent except for the faint lap of the water against stone.

She stilled completely, her shoulders locking tight, her breathing quick but shallow. I could see the tension in her frame, the churning war inside her between fear and something she likely couldn't name.

"Relax," I murmured, though I knew the word was foreign to her. My voice came softer than intended, a low rumble that settled into the space between us. She didn't flinch—good—but those brilliant green eyes tracked my every move.

I sank into the water, the temperature comfortably warm, not as scalding as I preferred. My wings folded inward, creating a faint ripple that reached her side, and I settled just close enough that we mirrored each other's height. She had no claws, no scales, her skin bare and fragile-looking in comparison, and still, she met my presence with an obstinate boldness that made the mate-bond pull even tighter.

I reached out slowly, careful not to startle her as I took her arm in my hand. Her skin was alarmingly smooth, so warm and delicate under my touch it felt like the barest whisper of sensation against my clawed fingers.

She stiffened but didn't pull away. That was a start.

With quiet precision, I lifted her hand and gestured out the expansive window overlooking the city. "Scalvaris," I said clearly, annunciating each syllable. I pointed across the vista of molten rivers and obsidian towers, my tone firm but unthreatening. "My city. Your new home."

Her eyes followed my gesture, her focus drawn to the pulsing life of Scalvaris below. For just a moment, awe replaced the fear and tension, softening her expression into something unguarded and raw. My chest swelled at the sight. My mate, alien and utterly foreign to my people, was looking at the city I ruled with the wonder of discovery. I would show her all of it.

But for now, simple gestures and intention would suffice. I pointed again to the training yards where warrior-screams echoed faintly through the haze of heat rising over stone and steel. "The combat pits," I rumbled. Then, I shifted my hand to the obsidian tower glinting just shy of the cavern roof's reach. "Our council."

Each word was deliberate, shared slowly, my tone even and unthreatening. She didn't understand the meaning, not fully, but her attention never wavered, her focus locked on both my gestures and my expression as though committing every detail to memory.

She was observant. That was all I could ask for now.

When I shifted to gesture again, her attention caught on the movement, and I felt her gaze dip— briefly but clearly—to my tail.

Ah.

Her frightened posture twitched like a flame. Not with pure terror. Something instinctual flared in her gaze, carefully muted by fear, but noticeable to someone as attuned to her every breath as I was.

No shame, no coy retreat. That tension I'd

noticed, the fire buried under that vulnerable surface, promised far more than mere resistance. It brought an ache to my groin, a patient, steady throb I longed to sink into her softness. But not yet. Not until she understood what she'd awakened.

I turned my head toward her again, leaning just a breath closer, tipping the balance between cautious distance and deliberate proximity. Her eyes snapped back up to mine, startled—the connection immediate.

My lips curved into a slow smile, and I felt a flicker of power shift between us.

"For now," I murmured, my tone quiet but heavy with intent, "you'll learn."

She wouldn't understand the words—but her gut instincts might. Those flashes of curiosity, the way her body reacted but didn't fully retreat, whispered to me of possibilities far greater than whatever distant stars birthed her.

One step at a time, my beautiful, fragile mate. I would teach her. About language, about trust, about belonging. About me.

I reached for the crystal fruit first, its translucent, glistening flesh catching the chamber's dim light. I held it in my claws and said the word clearly. "Krys-fruit." Turning to her slowly, I brought it to my mouth, taking a quick bite while keeping my eyes locked with hers.

She watched silently, her hands wrapped defensively around herself. I held the half-eaten fruit out to her, no words this time, just the offering. This was no trick. I didn't speak for her benefit, but for mine: "Krysfruit."

She didn't move at first. The tension between us lingered, thick as the heat of molten rock.

But after a long moment, she reached out slowly for the fruit, her wet fingers brushing the hard planes of my claws as if testing if I'd snap them closed like a trap. The soft contact of her skin against mine was electric and devastating. It stripped the air from my lungs, leaving only fire and smoke behind.

Mate. *Mine.*

Her lips parted slightly as she inspected the fruit, her mouth moving as though trying to form its name again. And then, without warning, she bit into it. Her breath hitched, and her eyes widened at the burst of flavor. Surprise colored her face, quickly replaced with something deeper—pleasure? Gratitude? It was fleeting, but I caught it. She inhaled deeply and finished it in two bites.

"Here," I growled softly, reaching for something else to distract from my rising instincts. "Redclaw," I explained, pulling it slowly from the tray. She mimicked the word, though her accent mangled it more than the last. I didn't care. Each broken syllable warmed me in ways I didn't think possible.

Piece by piece, she sampled the foods I handed her, every repetition of my language satisfyingly imperfect and wholly hers. The tension in her posture eased, her guard dropping under the weight of small kindnesses she clearly hadn't expected.

So when I reached to wipe the juice from her lower lip, the act surprised us both.

The angle of her jaw fit perfectly in my palm as I brushed the pad of my thumb against her skin, careful not to scratch her with my claw. Soft. Too soft for a warrior and yet utterly captivating. Warmth sparked across her flesh and into mine, lighting a fire that demanded to be fed.

Her lips trembled almost imperceptibly, her body leaning forward ever so slightly, a conflict she likely couldn't name flickering in those eyes.

She was aroused. And afraid.

I withdrew my hand before she could pull away, ripping my palm from her jaw with such force it was as if I were severing the bond itself. She blinked, the moment broken as confusion colored her features once more. The mate-bond screamed at the distance.

My discipline howled at the thought of pushing her too fast. I exhaled heavily, standing with my wings slightly mantled in frustration.

"Rest," I said gruffly, motioning to the food cart before kicking the impulse down further into silence. My gaze lingered just a second longer before I climbed out of the tub and stalked toward the adjoining chamber.

SIX

TERRA

After five freaking days of captivity that was unlike anything I'd ever encountered, I was going crazy. Darrokar kept me in his rooms. He fed me, sometimes *by hand*, and looked at me with desire clear enough to cross the galactic boundary of our species.

But he didn't try to touch me.

The bar was so low if I was thankful my alien captor wasn't a rapist.

I needed to get out of his rooms and do *something*. And, finally, the opportunity presented itself when Darrokar was called away by one of his men in a flurry of wings and weapons. It didn't look like he'd be back soon.

I'd been in plenty of hostile environments in my time. Cities brought to ruin by coordinated strikes.

Desert strongholds besieged by the enemy. Forests turned death traps by insurgents who knew the terrain better than they knew their own names.

But Scalvaris? This place was something else entirely.

It wasn't just the eerie beauty of it that unsettled me—or the fact that it was alien in every conceivable way. It was the pulse of the place, the way the underground river moved with purpose, the jagged obsidian towers looming like silent sentries, the faint vibration underfoot that hummed with a life of its own. The city wasn't just alive; it was watching.

So was he.

Even with Darrokar gone, I felt him everywhere. In the heavy air, the flicker of heat crystals set into the walls, the faint scent of something smoky and dark that clung to my skin after we'd shared that damned bath days ago. Distraction was a luxury I couldn't afford, and yet, there he was, burrowed under my skin.

I shook the thought loose, tightening the sash of the thin, draping garment Darrokar had left for me in the wardrobe. It felt too delicate on my skin, like I ought to be lounging in a palace and being hand fed grapes rather than skulking through this fortress of stone. The fabric shifted with every movement, whispering against my legs in infuriating contrast to the thick combat gear I was used to. But there wasn't time to curse my outfit.

I had a team to find.

Slipping out of Darrokar's private quarters had been easier than expected, though the tendrils of unease in the back of my mind warned me not to trust that. Doorways gave way to dark passageways, and I clung to those shadows like a thief, moving soundlessly as I'd been trained to do.

This wasn't just about survival. This was about Hawk, Kira, and the rest of the women who had trusted me with their lives. I hadn't heard from them since Darrokar dragged me into his world. Were they even alive?

I swallowed that thought before it could take root.

My boots—dry now, thankfully, after my stunt in the bath—muffled against the stone floor as I moved. Scalvaris unfolded around me, a labyrinth of volcanic beauty and alien architecture, no corner of it offering even the faintest illusion of safety.

The corridors opened onto a busy thoroughfare. Drakarn guards with pierced wings and painted claws stalked the perimeters while warriors sparred in open courtyards. Merchants bartered and bickered under glowing banners of some strange kind of fabric that shimmered like the skin of an oil slick. The air was thick—hot and metallic, tinged with the scent of scorched earth and something faintly sweet that might've been food.

I slipped into the crowd, keeping my head low and shoulders square, projecting an air of purpose. If you looked like you belonged somewhere, you could avoid most questions. It was a trick that worked for just about any Earth city. Alien strongholds, though? I had to hope it was a universal concept.

The Drakarn were taller than me—and broader —and their movements carried an innate predatory grace. I avoided their gazes as best I could, though I sensed the curiosity trailing me like a weighted cloak. No matter how I acted, I didn't look like I belonged.

Human female.

Alien.

I clenched my jaw against the wave of unease that followed.

Focus, Terra. Find your team.

I wasn't sure what we were going to do after that. It wasn't like we could repair our ship and go home, but I refused to remain a prisoner if there was anything I could do to fight back.

The buzz of voices around me rose and fell in

smooth rhythmic tones, words trading quick owner-ship between merchants and customers, guards and warriors, but the meaning filtered into my under-standing with startling clarity. It was almost scary how smoothly my translator worked.

"What's that thing?" a rough voice murmured nearby, low but sharp enough to cut through my thoughts.

I shifted subtly to glance at the source: two Drakarn warriors standing at a corner, their wings partially unfurled as though asserting dominance even in casual conversation. One of them tilted his head my way, just slightly, and I cursed silently.

"I've never seen anything like it," his companion said. "Who captured her? She isn't marked." There was an undertone of satisfaction that shot ice up my spine.

Just as the first warrior's eyes met mine, I stepped behind a passing merchant cart loaded with cloths and tools. *Remain calm. Keep moving.*

I ducked down an adjoining path, the atmosphere darkening with every step. The path sloped downward, leading me into a narrower corridor lit only by faint, intermittent glows from embedded crystals high above.

The din of the thoroughfare softened into

echoes, each step magnified in the enclosing walls. A mistake. I knew it almost immediately. I should've stayed in the open, however dangerous, rather than isolate myself in this predator's tunnel where sound carried but there was no easy road to escape if I was cornered.

A second footfall—definitely not mine—echoed faintly behind me.

I didn't react, forcing my heartbeat to steady even as adrenaline spiked painfully through my veins. Years of training distilled into each step, light and deliberate, drawing him closer without betraying my awareness.

If you run, you'll be prey.

The sound of claws scraping lightly against stone rippled down my spine. Guttural laughter followed, bouncing off the walls around me—a low, sinister chuckle that spoke of confidence, power, and the kind of cruelty that was clear despite the galactic distance.

I pivoted sharply, my fists already curling as I planted my feet. The Drakarn male—a hulking figure with slate-gray scales streaked in gold and crimson—saw my movement and paused just long enough to flash a smile that showed too many rows of jagged teeth.

"You shouldn't roam alone, little one," he said, his words rolling over me. The confidence in his tone made my skin prickle.

I straightened, letting my stance widen slightly. "I don't want trouble," I said, as if this were home; as if he could understand me.

The amusement in his gaze deepened. He unfurled his wings slowly, the leathery expanse brushing faintly against the walls of the corridor. "It gibbers." He stalked closer, each step deliberate. "You've strayed far, creature. Mine to take."

Take. The word hung in the air between us.

He lunged.

I pivoted on instinct, the move fast and sharp enough to sidestep him as his claws sliced through empty air. My fist shot out—fast and unforgiving—and collided with the side of his jaw. His scales absorbed the blow with far less impact than I hoped, but it was enough to stagger him for half a second.

Damn, that hurt my hand.

I couldn't hesitate. My heel slammed into the side of his knee, forcing his weight down, and I darted backward, aiming for distance.

He recovered too quickly. Wings moving like weapons in their own right, folding toward me as he surged upward in a flurry of movement. His claws caught the edge of my garment, tearing fabric as I twisted out of his grasp.

There was no way I could outmatch him in terms of strength. I had to be faster, smarter. My body moved on autopilot, muscle memory from years of training guiding me as I rolled beneath his second strike, the heat of his breath brushing my shoulder as I narrowly avoided his grip.

Pivot. Duck. Strike.

But his relentless speed sliced away any advantage I might have found. The narrow corridor funneled his larger frame directly toward me. He was built for this—pure, unyielding, ruthless. His claws slashed the air where I'd just been, close enough to stir the fine hairs on the back of my neck. I twisted away, only to have his tail snap outward, knocking my legs from under me. I hit the ground hard, air forced from my lungs in a sharp gasp.

Before I could recover, he was on me.

"So sweet, little morsel," he snarled, his voice as heavy and cloying as the heat pressing down on us. His claws dug into the stone on either side of me, trapping me between him and the coarse ground. His wings arched wide, cutting off the faint light above, bathing us both in shadow. "And I'll enjoy every—"

I bucked upward, slamming my knee into his

side. It wasn't much, but it made him grunt and shift his weight just enough for me to twist free—almost. His claws snatched at my wrist, his grip unrelenting as I struggled to wrench myself loose. I lashed out with my free hand, drove the edge of my palm toward his jaw, but he dodged it, the motion fluid, snake-like.

"Clever," he rumbled, flicking my arm aside with a calculated twist. He moved in a blur, pinning both of my wrists above my head in a vice grip that made my fingers go numb. With one hand, he immobilized me completely, his other trailing the torn edge of my garment. "But clever won't save you."

I thrashed against him, my breathing ragged as I pushed against his hold, but his strength was absolute, each attempt to get free like throwing myself against a wall of volcanic rock. Panic threatened to bubble to the surface, but I shoved it down, my mind racing for an opening.

He lowered his face toward mine, his fangs glinting faintly in the dim light. His breath was hot against my cheek, carrying the metallic tang of battle. "So fragile," he murmured, as though the revelation mystified him. His claws flexed slightly around my wrists, his intent a dark, coiling promise. "And yet your fire ... intoxicating."

Every nerve in my body screamed for action—for escape—but I was out of options. My muscles strained against the weight of him, fury and desperation coursing through me like a fever. His golden eyes glimmered with cruel amusement, drunk with the power imbalance.

"You will yield," he said, his voice dropping to a whisper, low and insidious.

"No," I spat, defiance laced into every fiber of my being. I didn't care if I couldn't win—I refused to let this bastard think he could break me. My teeth clenched in determination as I drove my knee into his stomach again. This time, he caught it with his own thigh, absorbing the impact fully. Shit.

He chuckled low, the sound vibrating through my bones. "Fight all you like, little one—"

His words ended in a choked gasp as something massive collided with him from above—a blur of obsidian scales and crimson eyes.

Darrokar.

Her scent hit me and everything else—the noise of the city, the heat of the air, the weight of duty—blurred into nothing but static.

Burning, intoxicating, *mine*.

The metallic tang of fear laced with the innate heat of her essence twisted through the corridor, jolting through my veins like a spark setting dry kindling ablaze. My claws flexed as I swooped down.

Every sense turned razor-sharp, every instinct narrowing down to a singular truth: someone had dared touch what was mine.

The crackle of my wings carried me forward, each beat concise, lethal. I didn't need to hear the snarl of a rival or the scrape of claws against stone;

the bond searing hot in my chest was enough. The scent of her fear pulling me deeper only hardened my resolve.

When I found him, whoever he was, I wouldn't leave enough of him behind to even be recognized.

The corridor opened below me, narrow and dim, like the throat of a predator swallowing prey. There she was—my woman. My mate. Pinned, pressed beneath the hulking frame of a fool whose arrogance would cost him his life.

The world stilled. Terra's red hair flashed in the dull glow of the crystals above, her eyes burning with anger even as her frame strained against the brute's grip. The torn fabric of her robe clung to her curves, a delicate temptation sharpened by the ferocious will radiating from her battered form. She wasn't broken.

Even now, caught in a moment where lesser creatures would yield, she fought.

I was moving before thought could catch up. My claws raked across the warrior's back as I descended. The satisfying crunch of impact and the guttural snarl torn from his throat barely registered—he flew forward and away from her like refuse cast aside. His body slammed into the opposite wall with a force that cracked the stone, but it wasn't enough.

Not nearly enough.

I was on him before he hit the ground, talons biting into his chest as I drove him down. My tail lashed, the sharp end snapping against him like a whip. His hiss of pain fed the storm inside me, an ember igniting into an unquenchable blaze.

"You touch what is mine," I growled, every word a vow of retribution. "You dare lay your filthy hands on her?"

The coward sputtered nonsense, claws scrambling at my grip, but he was drowning in the tide of my rage.

I struck him again—a clean, direct blow that shattered his jaw and muffled whatever plea he might've been foolish enough to voice. Blood spattered hot across the corridor floor, and still, he fought weakly against me, wings flapping once before falling limp.

More. The burning ran deeper than anger, deeper than instinct. This wasn't just about the affront to me—it was the threat to her. My mate. The risk he'd dared to take, the harm she might've suffered, and worse, the damage he'd already dealt, all fueled the fire ravaging me.

The tip of my claw trailed the hollow of his throat, and for a fraction of a moment, I weighed the balance of his life. It would be so easy—just a flick of my wrist, a casual slice, and any insult he'd ever dared breathe would vanish in the pool of his own lifeblood.

"Darrokar."

The steady voice was ice over flame.

I stiffened, my head snapping up. Rath stood at the end of the corridor, his ruby-red scales darkened by the dim light, his golden eyes steady and unfaltering in their appraisal.

"Enough," he said, his voice low, firm. "You're not a feral beast to fight over scraps."

Scraps?

I let out a snarl that vibrated through the floor beneath us. But behind the instinctual anger was the truth of his words cutting deep.

I shouldn't be standing over this pathetic excuse for a warrior like an enraged adolescent. Every action, every blow, every breath I took had repercussions—ones that extended far beyond my own satisfaction. Rath was not just one of my trusted lieutenants; he was one of the few who dared speak sense to me when I needed it most.

Sucking in a breath, I reined in the fire still snarling at the edges of my control. My claws retracted slowly, the scent of blood cooling.

But it wasn't over.

I snarled down at the crumpled pile beneath me. "You'll answer for this." The threat in my tone was marked not by an immediate promise of death, but by something colder—and far worse.

I straightened, chest heaving, and turned toward her.

Terra.

Her name branded itself in my mind even before my eyes found hers. She was on her feet now, leaning slightly against the wall for balance, but her stance was still as strong as before. Despite the reddening mark on her wrist, the tear in her robe, the undeniable evidence of her struggle, she didn't cower.

Her eyes blazed, filled with an emotion I couldn't quite place—fear? Fury? Something else entirely?

I closed the distance between us in two strides, folding my wings tight to keep from brushing against the jagged walls. My shadow spilled across her as I approached, and some treacherous part of me ... paused.

What would I find? Gratitude? Hatred?

The beast inside me wanted her caged against my chest, nestled beneath my wings, breathing my scent until she knew without doubt that I would annihilate anyone who dared come near her. The man within me—the leader, the lord—hesitated. The expression in her eyes didn't have a hint of submission.

It never had, not from the moment we'd first locked gazes back on the surface.

"Are you hurt?" The question left my lips before I'd meant it to, edged with more anger than worry. Not at her—at myself, for failing to stop this. She was still grasping my language, but she was learning almost unnaturally quickly. Perhaps a quirk of her alien species.

Her chin lifted. "Sivanae." *I'm fine.*

Spirit.

Heat roared to life beneath my scales once more, but this time, it wasn't anger. My claws curled slightly, the urge to soothe her quieting the violent edge lingering in my veins. I studied her wrist and stepped closer, my fingers grazing the images already burned into my mind—scents, textures, the heat that pulsed just below the surface of her human skin.

She didn't pull away. Didn't flinch. If anything, the awareness crackling between us deepened.

If Rath wasn't still somewhere nearby, I'd be tempted to take her against the stone wall.

"You shouldn't have left my quarters," I said, my voice low, restrained.

She arched a brow and opened her mouth, sucking in a breath. But she closed her lips and let the breath out without saying a word.

The tension between us was a living thing. Her gaze didn't waver, defiant even in the face of the heat building between us.

My fangs ached again, my wings radiated heat from unused energy, and most unsettling of all, I could feel her—*truly* feel her—in a way that went beyond the physical. It was as if her bravery, her fire, was threading itself into me, entwining with instincts I'd thought I could control.

She wasn't just a flame; she was an inferno, and I wanted to be consumed.

But now was not the time.

"Rath," I growled without turning away from her. My voice carried through the corridor, echoing with the sliver of authority I'd fought to recapture after my outburst. "Take care of him."

Rath stepped forward, his heavy claws clicking against the stone. The glow of his pupils shifted toward the crumpled warrior still struggling to rise from the floor. Rath didn't need to say anything. His gaze alone promised the kind of reckoning that would leave both scars and stories.

The injured male coughed, blood speckling his

lips, and attempted to spit out a few words. Whatever pathetic excuse or plea he hoped to offer never left his mouth. Rath seized him by the arm, wrenching him upright with a strength that belied his calm demeanor.

"Your orders?" Rath asked me, his tone neutral, but his eyes glinted with the expectation of blood.

"Banishment," I said, the words clipped, deliberate. I would have flayed the skin from his bones for what he tried, but Rath was right. We had rules here. Laws. And I had my duty. "If he sets foot here again, his life is forfeit."

Rath nodded once. He knew as well as I did that this couldn't be about my personal vengeance or the insult to Terra—this had to be about Scalvaris, the council, the laws that bound us.

Still, the beast inside me seethed, unhappy to let the matter go so easily.

Rath dragged the warrior down the corridor, his claws digging into his captive's shoulder with enough force to make him limp. The sounds of their retreat faded, leaving only the faint vibration of my breathing and the subtle crackle of heat crystals above.

I turned back to Terra.

She stood there, her shoulders squared, her chin

tilted up in that infuriatingly stubborn way that made it impossible to look away. Her fire was undimmed, even after what she'd endured. Perhaps even because of it. The faint tear in her robe revealed a sliver of thigh, her skin marred by a scrape that sent a fresh wave of fury surging through me.

My claws flexed involuntarily at my sides, aching for something—someone—to shred, but there was no one left to punish.

Not here. Not now.

She stared up at me, unflinching. She was a strange, fragile-looking creature by Drakarn standards, but in that moment, she felt as indomitable as the crystal peaks of Volcaryth. My mate.

"Why?" I demanded, the single word cutting through the silence like the edge of my blade. My voice came out rough, still jagged with the remnants of my rage. I repeated one of the few words she had learned in my tongue. "Why?"

She folded her arms across her chest, her movements tight and deliberate, as if shielding herself from the weight of my anger. She didn't answer, not in words.

Instead, she looked past me, her jaw tight, her throat working as she swallowed. Anger flared in me, unbidden and illogical. She wouldn't even meet my eyes. After all I'd just done—after I'd torn apart that bastard for daring to touch her—she stood there, defiant and distant.

I stepped closer, the heat from my body radiating between us. I wanted her to look at me. Needed it. For all her fire, her courage, her maddening refusal to submit, there was something about her silence that was ... unbearable.

I lifted my hand to her cheek, my claws careful not to hurt her delicate skin. She was warm beneath my touch, nothing like the rage simmering in me. She flinched, just barely, but didn't pull away. That defiance of hers again—burning, stubborn, and maddeningly intoxicating. She hadn't submitted to the bastard who had dared to touch her, and she wouldn't submit to me, either. Not without a fight.

Good.

"Why?" I repeated, softer this time, but no less demanding. My thumb traced the line of her jaw, brushing against the faint smudge of blood that wasn't hers. The sight of it made my wings twitch.

My mate—my woman—had been hurt in my city, under my watch. The guilt clawed at me as fiercely as the rage had moments ago.

Her eyes finally snapped to mine, sharp and unrelenting as a blade's edge. She said nothing, but the tension in her posture spoke volumes. She was angry—at me, at this place, at the circumstances that had forced her into this position.

"Do you seek to test me, fierce one?" I asked, my voice low, a dangerous rumble that carried more than a hint of warning. "I've already had to restrain myself once today. Do not tempt me to lose control again."

Her lips pressed into a thin line, but I saw the spark in her eyes—the spark that told me she was on the verge of spitting something back at me. She didn't, though. Instead, she tore her gaze from mine and yanked her arm free of my touch, turning her back to me in a deliberate act of rebellion.

The air between us crackled with tension, thick and suffocating. My claws twitched at my sides, and my wings unfurled slightly, the instinct to dominate, to claim, warring with the rationality that told me *not now*.

"You think you're strong enough to walk these halls alone?" I growled, stepping around her to block her path. "You think your ferocity will protect you from men like him?"

Her eyebrows scrunched together, and she opened her mouth again, hesitating over the words. "Warrior. Me. Fight."

It took me a moment to understand, and everything within me rebelled at the thought. I didn't want a weak mate. I'd always assumed my heart would one day belong to another warrior.

But Terra had no claws to slash, no scales to protect her, no wings. She was more helpless than the lowliest servant.

And had a warrior's fire in her heart.

Could I really deny her this?

"You want to fight, luvae?" I let the word slip before I could stop myself. *Luvae*. Not just "woman." Not just "mine." Something far more intimate. A word reserved for a bond so deep it was carved into a Drakarn's very bones.

A mate. *My* mate.

Her eyes narrowed, the sharp green of them cutting through the dim light like a blade. She didn't understand the word fully—she couldn't. But she recognized the weight of it, the way it lingered between us like the heat hanging in the thick air of Scalvaris.

"I fight," she said, her voice hard, clipped. She jabbed a finger against her chest, her meaning clear despite the fractured language. "Me. Warrior."

My wings flared slightly, a reflexive response to her audacity. The fire in her words made my blood simmer, equal parts frustration and something darker, hotter. I stepped closer, towering over her, forcing her to tilt her chin up to meet my gaze.

"You think you understand what it means to be a warrior?" My voice rumbled low, the cavern amplifying the menace woven into my words.

"Training begins tomorrow."

EIGHT

TERRA

The training area was everything I'd come to expect from the Drakarn: brutal, functional, and entirely unforgiving. Rough stone walls glimmered faintly in the light cast by heat crystals embedded in the ceiling. Their glow painted the cavern in molten oranges and reds, making the space look like it had been carved directly out of a volcano. The floor was worn smooth in some places, jagged in others, as if even the ground here would punish the unsteady.

A place like this didn't care about mercy. And neither did the man pacing in front of me.

Darrokar moved with all the lethal grace I'd come to associate with him: dark wings half-unfurled, casting jagged shadows that danced along the walls. His tail lashed in sharp, deliberate arcs, its spiked tip threatening to slice through the air between us. His claws flexed and curled as though itching for violence.

But it was his eyes—those molten gold, slit-pupiled eyes—that held me captive. Anger blazed within them like a forge stoked too hot, but there was something more, something darker writhing just beneath the surface.

"Disgrace," he snarled, his voice a low rumble that resonated through the cavern. The word ricocheted off the stone walls, its weight as sharp as his claws. "To attack one not marked as warrior. No honor."

I watched him, forcing myself to remain still. Observing. Calculating. If I was going to survive there, I needed to understand these people—their rules, their fragile egos, their ideology. And right then, I was learning a lot about what made Darrokar tick.

He wasn't just angry about my unsanctioned expedition into the lower tunnels. No, this was something deeper. Personal.

"The punishment is exile," he continued, the words more to himself than to me. His tail slammed once against the ground, sending a vibration through the floor strong enough to rattle my teeth. "But it should have been death. It *would* have been death—if—" He cut himself off, his teeth clicking together audibly.

That barely reigned fury of his could've suffocated weaker prey. But I wasn't prey. Not his. Not anyone's.

"Why did you leave?" he snapped suddenly, spinning to face me. His wings flared wide, nearly brushing the walls on either side of us. It was a deliberately intimidating display, but I refused to flinch. "Why risk—why go?" His words were clipped, as though speaking simply, hoping I would understand, cost him effort. His control was slipping by the second, and I couldn't shake how those seething remnants of anger lingered alongside something far less definable.

I pulled in a breath, readying myself for what I was about to say. My mask of control was thin, but I wore it like armor. "Because I needed to," I said evenly. With the translator's help, I'd picked up a lot of his language, even if it wasn't programmed to help me speak. "And I'm not helpless."

His eyes widened, a flicker of surprise cracking through his glowering mask.

"I won't let you cage me."

The resulting silence was deafening. He froze

mid-breath, tension coiling through his massive frame like an earthquake gearing up to strike. Slowly, deliberately, his wings folded back against his spine, and his gaze locked onto mine with renewed intensity.

"You speak our words," he said, the syllables slow and measured. His breath hitched, almost imperceptibly, as though he'd walked into an ambush deeper than he could have anticipated. "All this time, you understood?"

"Long enough," I replied, meeting his stare head-on. "I wanted to hear what you'd say when you didn't think I could understand."

"Clever," he bit out. The word dripped with distaste. And yet, beneath the disapproval, there was something dangerously close to admiration. "You should've stayed inside," he said finally, his voice losing some of its heat but none of its growl. "You are —" He paused, seeking the translation in his mind. "—too valuable to risk. Reckless."

"I don't need your protection," I said. The sharpness of my words sliced between us. "I'm a soldier—a warrior. Back on Earth, I led people into battles you couldn't begin to imagine. I *protected* them when no one else would. My people. My team. That's who I am. Not some ... fragile ornament you get to keep locked in a room."

Golden eyes narrowed. He stepped closer, enough for the heat radiating from his body to waft over my skin. "You think this is about keeping you? Claiming you?" His voice dropped lower, a throaty growl that somehow vibrated against the hollow of my chest. "If I wanted to 'keep you,' little warrior, you'd already be mine."

The way those words lingered—low and rough and laced with something that burned hotter than anger—made my blood ignite in a way I didn't entirely welcome. I swallowed hard, refusing to let him see even an inch of ground. "Then *prove it.* Train me."

He stilled. For one tense moment, he seemed to loom even taller, darker, his shadow stretching long across the cavern floor. "Train you?" he repeated, a new note invading his voice. His wings shifted, sharp-edged feathers rustling faintly as his head tilted to study me again. "You hope to challenge me, human?"

"No," I said, the word delivered with pointed clarity. "I hope to survive. And if there's anyone in this goddamned cavern who knows how to fight like one of you, it's you."

Darrokar exhaled sharply through his nose. "Arrogant," he muttered, though there was almost ... approval in his tone. "But not wrong."

I'd barely registered the shift in his stance before he moved. One heartbeat he was standing several feet away, the next he was face-to-face with me, so close I could see the faint, bluish veins that webbed through the black scales along his collarbone's jagged ridges. His heat washed over me again, molten and all-consuming, dragging my pulse into dangerous territory.

"Then fight for it," he rumbled, his voice raw. "There is no training without pain. No victory without blood."

Good.

Darrokar didn't give me time to reply. A blur of black scales and wings filled my vision as his tail whipped toward my legs. I leapt back, barely missing the strike that would've sent me sprawling. His movements were fluid, natural—as if each muscle in his body answered to some ancient rhythm. There was no hesitation, no pause to predict his next move. He was testing me, and I knew damn well he wasn't going to make this easy.

Good. I didn't want easy.

He lunged again, faster this time, and I dropped

low, rolling under one of his outstretched wings. My shoulder scraped the rough stone of the floor, sending a spike of pain up my arm, but I ignored it, springing to my feet. Before I could fully regain my stance, he was already moving, his claws slicing through the charged air in a controlled strike—not close enough to hit me, but close enough to remind me how sharp they were.

"Your instincts ... they are not entirely pathetic," he growled, circling me. His tail lashed behind him, coiled energy barely held in check. "But instincts alone will not save you. Not here."

I matched his steps, refusing to let him hem me in. "Then maybe you should stop showing off and actually teach me something," I shot back, my breath coming faster than I would've liked. He wasn't even winded. Of course he wasn't.

The corner of his mouth curved upward, a flash of fangs against his obsidian-black scales. "A warrior should never beg for knowledge. Take it." There was a challenge in his voice, low and electric, and I hated how much it set my nerves on fire.

"I'm not begging," I said, narrowing my eyes. "I'm demanding."

Darrokar stopped, wings unfurling just enough to shadow me as he leaned forward, closing the distance between. His golden eyes glowed in the dim light, molten and unwavering as they fixed on mine. "Then demand it with more than words, *Terra*."

The sound of my name on his tongue hit me harder than any blow. It wrapped around me, resonating in a way that made my stomach tighten and my chest ache. But I shoved that feeling aside.

He moved again, and this time I was ready. As his hand came toward me, claws curving just enough to hook, I stepped inside his reach, deflecting the strike with my forearm. The impact jolted through me, and it became startlingly clear just how solid he was. Like striking steel wrapped in scales. But I didn't back down—I pivoted, grabbing for the ridges along his arm to use his momentum against him.

It almost worked.

Almost.

But then his tail snapped against my calf, throwing me off-balance. I stumbled, and in an instant, he had me pinned. One massive arm locked around my waist, yanking me flush against his chest while his other hand braced my forearm, holding it immobile. His heat seared into my back, and when he leaned close, the low, rumbling vibration of his growl buzzed through my skin like static electricity.

"You rely too much on technique without understanding your opponent," he murmured into my ear, his breath hot and smoky against my neck. His voice was calm now, almost uncomfortably so. "You fight to win. My kind fight to dominate."

"As if there's a difference," I said through gritted teeth, twisting in his grip. I managed to free one arm and jab my elbow back, aiming for what I assumed was a pressure point just below his ribs.

It didn't have the effect I wanted.

Instead of releasing me, Darrokar laughed—a low, predatory sound that sent a flicker of warning through my gut. "So you do have claws after all," he said, and then, so quickly I couldn't counter, he spun me around and pressed me back against one of the cavern walls. His wings flared, closing in like walls on either side of me, boxing me in. "But they're dull. You'd be dead before drawing blood."

The worst part wasn't the position—it was the way his gaze raked over me, a mixture of challenge and something far more dangerous. He wasn't just testing my combat skills anymore. He was testing *me*. Every nerve in my body felt strung tight, as if this wasn't a fight but a negotiation happening on some deeper, unspoken level.

"You think I'm done?" I spat, defiance burning

away the unwanted heat pooling low in my stomach. "This was round one."

Darrokar's fanged smile widened, and a pulse of something fierce flickered in his expression. "*Now* you sound like a warrior."

Using anger as fuel, I shoved at his chest. He allowed the motion to unbalance him, only slightly, but it was enough for me to duck beneath his arm and put distance between us again. My breaths became ragged, and I tightened my stance, forcing my body to obey even while my senses screamed at how *close* he still was.

"Faster," he said and then lunged, dropping to a crouch as he swiped low with his tail. I jumped to avoid it, but the movement shifted my balance just enough for him to catch me mid-air, claws skimming my side as he spun me around and pinned me again. This time, when his chest pressed to mine, the rough stone of the wall dug into my back, grounding me in an intimacy that felt explosive rather than suffocating.

His head dipped low, and for one impossible moment, I swore his lips were close enough to graze mine.

"What are you waiting for?" he whispered, a low

rumble laced with maddening satisfaction. "Prove me wrong, *Terra*. Show me you are more."

I was breathing too hard to answer, every muscle coiled and trembling beneath his unrelenting heat. And then—then he looked at me, really looked, and something unspoken passed between us. His hand, still braced against my arm, loosened slightly, his claws careful as if remembering how breakable I was. His tail, still coiled near my ankle, stilled.

The air between us was electric, charged not only with tension but something far deeper and infinitely more potent. My pulse thundered in my ears, drowning out the weight of unasked questions lingering between us.

"Fuck it," I muttered.

And then, like a dam breaking, I grabbed the back of his neck and yanked him forward, slamming my lips up to his in a kiss that tasted like battle and surrender all at once.

At first, Darrokar froze, a flash of surprise breaking through his storm-like intensity. But the hesitation lasted less than a heartbeat. Then he was kissing me back—ferociously, flawlessly, with a heat that burned away reason. His claws bit into the stone at my side, fingers caging me even as his wings swept forward, shielding me completely from the outside world.

A growl rose from deep in his throat, vibrating through his chest and into mine. His lips were hot and firm against mine, his fangs grazing the edge of my bottom lip just enough to make me pull him closer, tighter, like gravity wasn't strong enough to hold us together.

When I finally broke the kiss to breathe, we were both panting, bodies pressed so tightly there wasn't space for air between us.

"Little warrior," he rumbled, his voice laced with something I couldn't pin down.

"Time for round two."

I snaked my hand around his neck and pulled him close, crushing our mouths together. This time, there was no hesitation—just pure, unadulterated need colliding between us.

Darrokar's arms wrapped around me, one sliding low along my spine to pull me against him while the other tangled in my hair. The sharp tips of his claws scratched lightly at my scalp, sending a shiver rippling down my body that had nothing to do with fear and everything to do with lust.

I arched into him, relishing how hard he felt beneath his thin training pants.

A growl escaped him as I nipped at his bottom lip, catching it gently between my teeth before soothing the sting with a swipe of my tongue. He groaned, a low rumble from deep within his chest. It vibrated against my ribs and sent bolts of energy sparking through my veins.

He released his grip on my waist only to bring both hands up, cupping either side of my face. His thumbs stroked across my jawline, tracing its contours reverently. The touch was surprisingly tender considering that he had claws that could tear me to shreds with one wrong move.

"I've never wanted anything more than you," he murmured against my lips before dipping his head lower. His tongue traced a scorching path along my throat and collarbone while his fingers slid down over my shoulders until they reached the neckline of my borrowed armor top.

I sucked in a deep breath as those razor-sharp points trailed delicately across my skin. Even through the haze of desire, some distant corner of my brain marveled at how careful he was being with me.

There was only the hot stone of the training floor, and though this was Darrokar's private quarters, it wasn't exactly secluded. Anyone could walk in on us.

I couldn't care.

The world had narrowed to this moment: me, him, and his hands peeling away my clothes.

He tugged impatiently at the straps holding my armor together, fumbling clumsily with the fastenings in his haste to remove them from me entirely. Until, with a sexy growl, he tore through the straps with his claws, slicing them to ribbons.

If I had any survival instincts left, I'd be running right now. But it was too late. My pulse thundered against his lips.

"Terra ..." He whispered my name like a prayer as he pulled back far enough for our eyes to meet once more—and what I saw burning within their depths took my breath away completely.

It wasn't just lust or desire—it ran deeper than that somehow—older and wilder than anything I'd ever felt before in my life.

And it scared me how much I wanted it too.

His claws trailed down my sides, leaving goosebumps in their wake as he traced every curve and dip of my body before finally coming to rest upon my hips. He gripped them firmly, possessively, drawing me even closer until there wasn't so much as an inch separating us.

"*Luvae,*" he growled, lips pressing against my neck.

I didn't know exactly what it meant, even with the translator, even after he'd used it so many times, but the word sent a shiver down my spine. I tilted my head back, offering him better access. His tongue traced patterns across my skin, leaving trails of fire wherever it touched.

I was on the ground before I realized he was laying me down, my legs spread and his hips nestled between them, his heavy weight pinning me in place. I could feel the hard length of his cock straining against the fabric of his pants and pressing insistently between my thighs.

The stone of the training floor was hot against my naked back, and the heat of Darrokar above me only intensified the sensation. It should've been uncomfortable, maybe even painful, but instead, I found myself arching into it, craving more of the delicious friction that was building between us.

He shifted slightly, angling himself so that his hips rubbed against mine in a way that made stars burst behind my eyes. "More," I panted, reaching up to tangle my fingers in his thick, dark hair. He obliged, grinding against me, his movements slow and deliberate and utterly intoxicating.

His tail curled around one of my ankles, locking it in place while his claws hooked under my knee, lifting it higher, allowing him to tear my pants off until I was completely nude. His wings flared wide, casting shadows over us both.

Then he curled them in tight and grinned. "I want to devour you, *luvae*." He leaned down, and his lips captured one of my nipples. I gasped, arching against him as he teased it with his tongue, flicking and circling the sensitive peak until it hardened beneath his touch.

His tail flicked up between my thighs, caressing the slick folds there until it found my clit. The contact sent sparks dancing through me, making me buck helplessly against him.

He made a rumbly sound in his chest that vibrated against me, and I moaned shamelessly in response.

My breasts ached for him to pay attention to them, and he must've sensed it because his tongue licked a hot line from one nipple to the other before his teeth scraped across them, sending shivers of pleasure racing through my body. He sucked on one, then the other, drawing each tip between his fangs until they were swollen and sensitive.

I never thought I could come from just that, but he had me close.

His tail continued stroking my sex, coiling itself

between my thighs before plunging its smooth, scaled tip into me. It thrust in and out slowly, methodically, building the pressure inside me with every stroke. I was dripping with need, aching for more.

Holy fucking shit.

It was beyond unreal. And from the tone of Darrokar's dark, sensual laugh, it was only beginning.

Darrokar's tail withdrew from me, leaving me panting and reeling. I barely caught my breath before his hands were on me again, lifting and turning me onto my side. His powerful body moved with a graceful, predatory fluidity that captivated me.

"Look at me," he commanded in a voice rough with desire. His golden eyes glowed intensely, reflecting the dim, fiery light of the cavern. I obeyed, turning slightly to see him kneeling beside me, his wings arched behind him like dark, menacing arches.

He was an impressive sight—black scales gleaming with a reddish tint, muscles dancing under his skin as he moved, his erection straining against the now-far-too-tight fabric of his combat trousers.

He stripped them away, revealing his cock in all its alien perfection.

I was mesmerized by the sight, my earlier

curiosity now a blazing inferno of fascination. His penis was unlike anything human, with its base covered in black and red scales, transitioning into red flesh with thick, dark veins that throbbed. The tip was uncut, surrounded by a fleshy, tongue-like structure that moved independently, twitching in anticipation, as if inviting me closer.

A bead of liquid pearled at the tip, and without thinking, I reached out to touch it. My fingers brushed against the smooth, velvety surface, and his entire body shuddered. His whole cock was covered in a warm and slick fluid, nearly as wet as I was, and carrying his unique, intoxicating scent that made my head spin with desire.

"Terra ...," Darrokar murmured, his voice a mix of reverence and raw need.

I brought my hand to my lips, tasting him. The flavor was unexpected, musky and potent, laced with an aroma that seemed to seep into my very bones. My tongue, already overly sensitive, tingled with the contact, sending a wave of arousal straight through me.

"This is part of my pheromones," he said, watching me closely, his eyes dark with lust. "The more we do this, the more intense our arousal will grow. The harder it will be to stop."

There was no way I was stopping. Darrokar's gaze never left mine as he guided my hand to his erection, his cock already leaking pre-cum in antici-pation. I wrapped my fingers around it, marveling at the unique texture. It was warm to the touch, almost hot, and I could feel the pulse of his heartbeat in the thick veins. The scales along the base were surprisingly smooth, a subtle contrast to the ridged flesh above them.

As I began to stroke him, my thumb brushed over the intriguing tongue-like tip, sending a shiver down my spine. Darrokar's low growl vibrated through his body, his hips reflexively jerking into my touch with urgency. I teased the sensitive flesh, circling and stroking it in a rhythm that seemed to drive him wild, the obsidian scales at the base of his cock glinting in the dim light.

His pre-cum drooled steadily, smearing between my fingers and soaking into my palm, leaving a sticky trail. I leaned in, capturing the tip of his cock between my lips, and swirled my tongue around it to taste more of those intoxicating pheromones. They had a sharp, musky flavor, both familiar and unknown, fueling my own growing arousal.

Darrokar's fingers tangled in my hair, guiding my head as I lavished attention on his cock. His hips rocked into my mouth, using my rhythm to fuck himself against my tongue. The blunt, tongue-like tip bumped against the roof of my mouth, sending sparks through me with each touch.

I sucked harder, determined to wring every drop of pleasure from him.

His tail was between my legs again, stroking my folds until I was practically shaking. I moaned, the dual sensations of his cock in my mouth and his touch on my sex driving me wild.

Darrokar's wings flared, the shadows cast by their dark membrane dancing across the stone floor as he exhaled a ragged breath. His claws scraped against my shoulders, the slight pain mixing with the pleasure as I continued to explore him with my lips and tongue. I could feel the heat building between us, the air thick with the scent of us.

"Terra, your mouth ... fuck," he groaned. "I need to be inside you, *luvae.*"

My body ached for it.

With a grunt of effort, Darrokar flipped me onto my back, his powerful form pinning me to the stone floor. I wrapped my legs around his hips, feeling the thick head of his cock nudge against my entrance.

"Yes, please," I whispered, grinding against him

desperately. The heat of his body enveloped me, his scales rough against my sensitive skin.

His eyes blazed with an intense golden light as he gazed down at me, his pupils dilated to slits. The air between us was alive with raw, unbridled lust, the heat from his skin radiating against my own. "You're so wet for me, luvae," he panted, his deep, gravelly voice sending shivers down my spine. His tail curled possessively around my thigh, the tip dragging lightly over my sensitive skin, eliciting a whimper of pleasure from my lips.

I nodded frantically, unable to form words as my hands gripped his forearms, anchoring myself to him. I was lost in the hunger of the moment, drowning in my own desire that seemed to mirror his. The musky scent of his arousal filled my nostrils, a heady mix of male pheromones and something uniquely his that made my head spin and my core clench around emptiness.

With a low, vicious growl, Darrokar pushed forward, the thick, sensitive head of his cock breaching my slick entrance. I gasped, my back arching off the ground as he stretched me open with a deliberate, almost brutal slowness.

"Darrokar!" I cried out, and he sank deeper. He

paused, his hips still, giving me a moment to adjust to his size.

A wave of dizzying pleasure rippled through me as Darrokar's full length finally filled me, his cock pulsing with each beat of his heart. I was stuffed to the brim, every inch of him embedded deep within my core, his base pressed firmly against my sensitive clit.

The sensation of being so completely claimed by him, of his immense cock stretching me open in a way no human ever had, was overwhelming. It was like nothing I'd ever experienced, and my body responded with a desperate, primal urge to move, to take him even deeper.

Darrokar held himself there, buried inside me, the veins on his neck corded with tension as he fought for control. I wanted to feel him moving within me, the heavy thrusts I knew he was capable of, but instead, he stayed utterly still, as if giving me time to adjust to his overwhelming presence.

"Move ... please," I begged, my voice breaking on a desperate moan. "I need to feel you."

With a sharp, guttural growl, Darrokar surged forward, his hips snapping against mine in a relentless rhythm that stole my breath and shattered my control. He pounded into me with brutal efficiency, each thrust driving me deeper into the stone floor, the force of his movements rattling my bones.

The pleasure was intense, a blinding, all-consuming fire that ravaged my senses and left me mindless in its wake. I wrapped my legs tighter around his waist, using the leverage to meet his thrusts, to take him as deep as he could go. My nails raked down his back, leaving scored trails on his scales as I gripped him, holding on for dear life as he ravished me.

The sound of skin slapping against skin, punctuated by my ragged gasps and moans, filled the cavern. Darrokar's cock throbbed inside me, his thickness stretching me in ways that bordered on pain, but the pleasure far outweighed any discomfort. My inner walls clenched around him, milking his length as he pounded into me, the friction building with each merciless stroke.

"*Luvae*, I can feel you ... so close," Darrokar panted, his voice a rough growl. His golden eyes flickered with a feral glow, his gaze feverish and possessive as he watched me.

I could only moan incoherently, my body moving in time with his, seeking that exquisite release that eluded me. The pressure inside me built to a crescendo, my walls pulsing around his cock as he drove into me harder, faster.

And then, with a keening cry, I shattered. My orgasm ripped through me like a wildfire, consuming everything in its path. Wave after wave of bliss crashed over me, leaving me gasping and trembling in Darrokar's passionate grasp.

Darrokar's powerful body tensed, his muscles rippling beneath his scales as he buried himself to the hilt inside me. He groaned, a deep, carnal sound that vibrated past his chest and into mine. His cock throbbed, pulsating with a rhythmic intensity that seemed to synchronize with my own clenching release.

"I'm going to come," he warned, his voice strained with the effort of holding back. "Hold on, *luvae*."

With a guttural roar, he released, his hips jerking with each violent spasm as he emptied himself inside me. His hot seed flooded my core, coating my inner walls with a thick, viscous warmth. I felt every pulse, every tremor of his climax, the sensation almost unbearably intense as he filled me to the brim.

The heat of his release seared through me, intensifying the pleasure already coursing through my veins. I was helpless to do anything but surrender to the overwhelming sensations, my body wracked with the aftershocks of my own orgasm.

Darrokar nuzzled into my neck, repeating one word over and over. *"Luvae. Luvae. Luvae."*

And something in me finally understood. It didn't mean *mine*. Not exactly.

It meant mate.

TEN
DARROKAR

The air was heavy with her scent.

It wasn't just there in my chambers—it clung to my skin, my wings, my very senses. Sweet, wild, and utterly intoxicating, it overpowered the tang of molten stone and heat crystals embedded in the walls. It blurred the dividing lines of my thoughts, drowning out every instinct except the unshakable knowledge that she was mine.

Terra Drake. Human. Warrior.

Mate.

My bond to her was no longer an unfulfilled ache—it was real now, visceral, carved into the marrow of my bones. Every beat of my heart pulsed with it, this connection between us, fierce as fire and as unrelenting as the world outside these walls.

She had fought me—challenged me—and I had claimed her.

But even now, as she lay curled against me, her breaths steady and deep with sleep, I knew this bond was not so simple. She was no fragile thing, no docile creature content to be tamed. No, she burned with a fire that refused to be extinguished.

And it was that fire that both drew me to her and unsettled me more than I cared to admit.

I stretched across the smooth, heat-warmed stone of my sleeping platform, my wings draping over its edges like smoldering shadows. Its surface, carved from volcanic rock, radiated the comforting warmth of my people's fire-born home. Around me, my chambers glowed faintly with light from the heat crystals, their molten orange veins crawling through the blackened stone like living things. Shadows flickered across the ceiling, the dance of firelight a reflection of the restless energy pulsing through me.

She stirred beside me, her copper hair spilling across my obsidian scales in a cascade of molten light. Her hand rested against my ribcage, delicate fingers curling as if she sought to anchor herself to me even in sleep. Her warmth sank into me, more potent than the heat that surrounded us.

I should have let her rest. Should have allowed

her this brief reprieve from the chaos of this world that was not her own. But responsibilities loomed beyond these walls—duties that would not wait, threats that would not yield. My people. My enemies. The council. All of them circled like carrion birds, waiting for any sign of weakness, any crack in my armor. And Terra ... Terra was no ordinary crack. She was a blaze, wild and beautiful, and I knew it would take all my strength to shield her from what was to come.

A faint shift in the chamber's light caught my attention. The massive doors at the far end, carved with the sigils of my house, groaned open with deliberate slowness. A figure stepped inside, silhouetted against the low glow of the hall beyond. Tall, crimson-scaled, and exuding the confidence of a predator who knew his place in the hierarchy.

Rath.

He entered without hesitation, his wings tucked neatly against his back and his molten ruby-red scales shimmering faintly in the light. His sharp amber eyes swept the room, lingering briefly on the sleeping form of Terra before meeting mine. His mouth curved into a smirk—the kind that had earned him more than one scar in his years as my subordinate.

"Darrokar," he greeted, his voice low and rough. "I see you've been … busy."

I rose slowly, careful not to disturb Terra. Her hand slipped from my chest as I shifted, and though her warmth lingered, the absence left a quiet ache in its wake. She murmured something soft, a garbled word that I couldn't quite catch, before settling once more into stillness.

"Speak," I ordered Rath, my voice low and clipped. My wings flared slightly as I stepped away from the platform, the movement stirring the heavy air of the chamber. "And make it quick."

Rath's smirk widened as he came closer, his taloned feet clicking softly against the stone floor. "The exile is done," he said simply, his tone casual. "The *kervash* won't find shelter in the wastes. And if he does, it won't last long."

A growl rumbled deep in my chest at the memory of that bastard's audacity. His hands on Terra, his challenge to my claim—it had taken more restraint than I cared to admit not to end him myself. My claws flexed, scraping against the stone. "Good," I said darkly. "If he values his life, he'll stay gone."

Rath nodded, though the gleam in his eyes told me he hoped to meet the *kervash* again. "And if he doesn't, I'll gladly remind him why that was a mistake."

The words might have been a joke, but his gaze drifted again to Terra, and though there was no malice in his curiosity, it still set my instincts on edge. I stepped closer, my wings flaring wider in a reflexive show of dominance.

"She's ... different," Rath said at last, tilting his head as he regarded her. His tone was cautious, but not entirely free of judgment. "Not what I expected."

"You expected nothing," I snapped, my voice sharp as the edge of a blade. "You know nothing of her."

Rath raised his hands in mock surrender, the smirk fading from his face. "The council will want to know more," he said carefully. "You know they'll question this. Question her."

"Let them," I growled, stepping closer. The heat of my anger flared in the air between us. "I have no interest in their doubts or their traditions. Terra is mine, and no council, no law, will take her from me."

Rath studied me for a long moment, his amber eyes narrowing slightly. "Traditions run deep, Darrokar," he said quietly. "You've always walked the line between honoring and defying them. Just be certain which side you stand on."

I didn't respond. I held Rath's gaze, the weight of his words settling uneasily in my chest. Loyalty was etched into his bones, but his caution was not without merit. The council would not let this go unchallenged. They would see Terra as a disruption, an unknown, perhaps even a threat. And to them, threats were meant to be eliminated.

But the fire that burned within me—the bond that tethered us—was unshakable. Terra was no threat. She was strength. Resilience. Defiance. And she was mine.

Rath must have sensed the resolve in my silence, for he shifted, his wings folding more tightly against his back. "For what it's worth," he said, tilting his head, "I've never seen you like this. It's ... unsettling."

I narrowed my eyes. "Unsettling?"

He nodded, his smirk returning, though it lacked its earlier edge. "You're quieter. Less ... predictable. Whatever she's done, it's making the rest of us nervous."

"Good," I said, my voice low and deliberate. "You should be nervous."

Rath gave a short laugh, more breath than sound, and inclined his head. "As you say, Warrior Lord.

But nervous warriors make rash decisions. Keep an eye on your council—they'll be watching."

Without another word, he turned and strode toward the door, the click of his talons echoing off the chamber walls. His wings brushed lightly against the frame, and the heavy door groaned shut behind him, leaving me alone with my mate once more.

I stood there for a moment, staring at the closed door, my thoughts uneasy. Rath's words were an unwelcome specter in the back of my mind. He was right—nervous warriors did make rash choices. And the council was nothing if not a collection of nervous old fools.

But I would deal with them if and when they became a problem. For now, my priority was here— beside me, stretched across the sleeping platform like she belonged in this world carved from fire and stone.

"Who was that?" Terra's voice startled me, soft but steady, tinged with curiosity.

She was propped up on one elbow. The red waves of her hair framed her face, and her green eyes glinted with humor. She was watching me closely, her gaze as sharp as ever. She was my mate; I should have expected nothing less.

"Rath," I said simply, crossing the room to stand beside her. "A warrior. And a nuisance."

She laughed softly, a sound that sent a pleasant hum through my chest. "I figured as much," she said, stretching languidly. "He came to poke the bear."

I tilted my head, frowning. "What? What is a bear?"

Her lips twitched into a grin that was part teasing and part affection. "Large, furry predator. Very grumpy. Not unlike you."

A low growl rumbled in my throat, but there was no heat behind it. I leaned closer, bracing one hand on the platform beside her, my wings shifting slightly to block out the faint glow of the heat crystals. "Grumpy?" I murmured, my voice a dangerous purr. "You think I am grumpy, little warrior?"

Her smile widened, unafraid of the dark promise in my tone. If anything, she seemed to enjoy provoking me. "Absolutely," she said, her voice laced with humor. "Don't worry—I like it. In a terrifying, 'don't-mess-with-me-or-I'll-breathe-fire' kind of way."

I couldn't help the faint smirk that tugged at my lips. Her courage, her sharp wit—it never failed to catch me off guard. "I don't breathe fire."

She reached up, her fingers brushing lightly

against my jaw, her touch soft yet electrifying. "No?" she asked.

The air between us crackled, charged with something stronger than the mating bond. The heat of the room, the glow of the crystals, the distant hum of the geothermal currents—it all faded into the background.

There was only her. Her fire. Her defiance.

I caught her hand in mine, my claws brushing against her smaller, softer fingers. The difference between us—her fragility, my strength—should have been stark. Irreconcilable. And yet, it didn't matter. Because in that moment, she wasn't fragile. She was unshakable.

"You are a menace," I muttered, though the words held no bite.

"And you love it," she countered without missing a beat, her grin widening.

I didn't respond, but the look in her eyes told me she already knew the answer. She always seemed to know.

She shifted slightly, pulling herself up to sit cross-legged on the platform. Her copper hair caught the flickering light, turning it into a halo of flame. "So," she said, her tone more serious now. "What's the plan?"

I raised an eyebrow. "The plan?"

"Yes, Darrokar, the plan," she said, rolling her eyes. "You don't strike me as the kind of guy to just wing it."

I flicked my wings just enough to let them catch the light. "Winging it has worked well enough for you so far."

She smirked. "Of course."

I growled softly, though the corners of my mouth twitched. "I make no promises."

Her expression softened, and the humor faded, replaced by something quieter. "I'm serious," she said, her voice quieter now. "This bond between us— it's ... intense. And I can see it in your eyes. Is there something I'm missing here?"

"It's my responsibility to protect you," I said simply, as if that could encompass the depth of what I felt.

She shook her head, her expression firm. "I can take care of myself."

"You are mine, *luvae*."

Before she could start to argue, I captured her lips and lowered her back to the sleeping platform. We had no need for more words.

ELEVEN
TERRA

If there was one good thing about dating—could you call it dating? —the scary Drakarn leader, it was that I no longer had to sneak around to find my people. I just had to ask.

But as one of Darrokar's warrior trainees lead me through narrow passages and down deep into the caverns of Scalvaris, my wariness grew. It wasn't just because of the attack. After training sessions with Darrokar, I had more than one way to get away from an attacker, but my brain still had to catch up with that.

It was dark down there, the crystals in the walls glowing so dim I had to squint to see, and I didn't spot the door until my guide came to a halt.

I stepped inside, expecting the worst.

This wasn't where they'd kept us before, and once I was through the door, it wasn't *that* bad. It was brighter, for one, and there was furniture.

The room was carved entirely from stone, the furniture sleek and functional, with chairs and low tables molded from the same obsidian-like material. A larger table in the corner hosted scattered supplies—rations, some clothing, and a few unfamiliar tools. Despite the relative comfort, it was clear that while this wasn't a dungeon, it wasn't exactly freedom either.

Hawk was the first to notice me. She rose quickly from her seat at the corner table, her tall frame unmistakable even in the dim light. The sharp intake of her breath was followed by a burst of motion as Kira and Vega turned toward the door. The flickering light cast their expressions in shifting shadows—relief, disbelief, and something sharper beneath the surface.

"Captain," Hawk said, her voice tight with suppressed emotion. She didn't need to call me that, but she must have been shaken if it slipped out. It wasn't a title we used for familiarity there, but hearing it made my stomach twist into knots. "You're not dead."

I couldn't help the smallest, hollow smile. "Not

quite," I said, keeping my tone light to mask the weight beneath it. As I stepped farther into the room, the atmosphere shifted. Where there had been relief, suspicion began to take root. One by one, they straightened, their eyes narrowing as they took me in.

"Where the hell have you been?" Vega's voice broke the silence, a low growl of frustration barely restrained. Her arms were crossed tightly over her chest, her muscular frame rigid with tension. Her eyes shone with accusation as they met mine.

"I wasn't exactly able to move around the city," I said firmly, though their reactions were fair; I would've felt the same. My voice was even, commanding, but my own guilt clawed at the edges of my composure. "It's complicated—the Drakarn don't trust us."

She raised an eyebrow, the faintest smirk lifting one corner of her mouth, but it wasn't amusement—it was cold calculation. "Complicated? That's an impressive way to describe leaving your team stranded," she said, her words deliberately measured, barbed just enough to land their hit but not too much to be insubordinate.

My grip tightened on the edge of one of the stone chairs as I stepped fully into the room and allowed the heavy door to close behind me. "Stranded? As if I had a choice to leave you! I've been trying to find you guys for two weeks."

"That's rich," Hawk muttered sharply, coming to stand beside Vega. The two loomed like a united front, their solidarity almost tangible. "We've been dragged around this place like cattle, interrogated repeatedly despite the fact it's clear we don't speak the language, and watched day and night by freaking alien dragon-monsters who act like we're a zoo exhibit. Where the hell have you been?"

I flinched, my soldier's mask cracking just a fraction.

"I didn't have a choice." My reply came softer than I intended, and that was a mistake. Hawk seized on it immediately.

"No choice? Or did you just find a cozy place with a bit less stone and a bit more ..." Her words trailed off, her expression darkening. Her gaze flickered to the leather vambrace around my arm.

Vega pounced on Hawk's unspoken insinuation. "Yeah, you look remarkably ... well-fed. Well-rested." Her eyes flicked between me and the door, as though expecting someone to burst in after me uninvited. "And those clothes ..."

My team looked clean enough; clearly, they'd managed to bathe at some point, and their clothes weren't as ragged as you'd expect after two weeks, so they might have been washed. But they weren't in the borrowed warrior leathers I was wearing.

"Don't," I snapped sharply, my voice ringing out in a way that silenced them all. The effect was momentary, but the words had done their job. I drew in a slow breath and composed myself before continuing. "This place isn't what we could have expected. Darrokar—"

A collective groan interrupted me the moment I'd spoken his name. Hawk threw up her hands, and Vega's smirk turned positively venomous. "Oh, here it is," she muttered. "She's dicknotized."

"I'm not dicknotized!" I said, louder than I should have. My voice momentarily startled even me, echoing faintly against the walls. My cheeks burned with a blush, and I wanted to bury my face in my hands.

Hawk's jaw dropped slightly, her dark eyes narrowing with something a lot like realization—and betrayal. "Oh my God," she said flatly. "Are you really ... How do you even with the claws?"

Heat bloomed in my chest. "Carefully. Guys, it's not what it sounds like. Darrokar is—"

"Different?" Vega scoffed. Her cold, gray eyes

sparkled with disbelief. "You've got to be kidding me, Terra."

"You don't understand," I snapped, rounding on her sharply enough that even Vega seemed taken aback. "I've been learning all I can about this place. It's not like we have any other place to go. We need to figure out how to make a life here."

"So are we all shacking up with scary aliens?" Kira muttered from her seat near the window. Unlike the others, her tone lacked venom, but her quiet detachment was worse.

I turned to her sharply, hoping for an opening to better understand her uncharacteristic demeanor, but the rest of the team wasn't about to let the conversation die.

"Men don't just help powerless women for free, Captain. I don't think it matters what planet you're on," Hawk said evenly, pointedly using the title again with all the weight of an accusation.

I couldn't respond—not the way they wanted me to. The truth was too tangled, too raw to share without unraveling it completely. "We're alive," I said flatly. "That's what matters."

The tension in the room thickened with every second of silence that followed. They didn't trust me —not completely. I couldn't blame them, but that didn't mean I had the luxury of indulging their doubts. We didn't have time for division.

"We need a plan," Vega said suddenly, breaking the stalemate with her usual pragmatism. She straightened, stepping forward just enough to draw attention back to her. "This situation, whatever arrangement you think you've made—it's a temporary solution at best. We need to take control of our circumstances before we lose any chance."

Hawk nodded in agreement, but Kira remained silent. Her focus seemed fixed on some invisible point beyond the barred window, her body language distant and closed. I filed it away for later—something was definitely off.

"And what do you propose we do?" I asked, crossing my arms and tilting my head expectantly.

Vega's lips curved upward into a faint smile, but there was no humor in it. "We need to be in a less secure location, for one."

"I think I can get you moved to better quarters." No matter what Vega was planning, it was on my list. My team shouldn't be prisoners.

"That's step one," Vega continued. "Then I slip out and find the others. It's all well and good that you've found a boyfriend, but have you forgotten the civilians we're supposed to be protecting?"

"I have not," I said, my tone sharp. "But we need to stop acting hostile. If you let me tell Darrokar—"

"Absolutely not!"

"No way."

"Are you crazy?"

It was a unanimous no.

"You're assuming we're not already considered threats," Vega countered, holding my gaze without flinching. "Do you really think they'll let us move freely?" She tilted her head towards the door where my escort was waiting outside.

Kira finally spoke, her voice cutting through Vega's as if on cue. "And if the others are dead?"

The bluntness of her words struck the room like a blade, silencing everyone. Even Vega faltered, her mouth closing into a thin line.

"They're not dead," I said firmly, though the knot in my chest tightened at the thought. "We can't think like that. If there's even a chance—"

"If they're gone, Terra. What then?" Kira pressed. She still wasn't looking at me directly, but her words carried an edge I wasn't used to hearing from her.

"Then we mourn but keep going," I said forcefully. "And we need to remain together to do that."

"Are we together?" Hawk asked quietly but pointedly. Her words weren't loud, yet they landed with the weight of an avalanche. The unspoken question hung in the air: *Are you with us, or are you with **him**?*

I drew a breath, my gaze sweeping over each of them before returning to Kira's still-guarded expression. I didn't have the answer they wanted—but maybe I could give them something else.

"I am still with you," I said finally, my voice quiet but firm. "And I swear, I will find a way to get us out of this hell. But if we screw this up and Darrokar—"

"What are his intentions exactly?" Hawk pressed, her tone skeptical. "As far as I can tell, all we've earned for two weeks of patience is this room and a lot of unanswered questions."

The truth burned at the back of my throat, but I couldn't give them that yet. Instead, I kept my voice calm, even. "Give me time."

Vega shook her head but didn't argue further. She turned toward the table, busying herself with organizing supplies. Hawk followed Vega's lead, rummaging through the makeshift inventory with ill-concealed frustration.

Only Kira lingered near the narrow window, her distant gaze unreadable.

As my team settled reluctantly into tense silence, I stepped closer to her, my expression softening just enough to pass as nonchalant. "Kira," I said softly. "What's going on?"

She hesitated before answering, her shoulders stiffening slightly. "Nothing. Just thinking."

"Anything I should know?"

Her eyes flicked toward me briefly, but she didn't hold my gaze. "No," she replied quickly—too quickly.

I studied her for a moment longer, debating whether to push harder. But something in her posture warned me against it. Kira wasn't ready to talk, and forcing the issue would only make it worse.

"Alright," I said finally, stepping back and allowing her the space she clearly wanted. But as I turned away, her quiet urgency echoed in my mind, along with Vega's cold practicality and Hawk's frustrated skepticism.

They were my team, my people—and I'd never felt more separate from them.

I had walked into this room expecting to reunite with familiar camaraderie, with strength forged in shared struggle. But all I'd found were fault lines, cracks that spiderwebbed deeper than any one conversation could bridge.

I had to fix this.

Somehow.

TWELVE

TERRA

Everyone made sacrifices for survival—sometimes it was dignity, sometimes it was trust. I wasn't sure which I was losing more of lately. The echo of my team's words from earlier still rang in my ears, sharp as a combat knife.

It didn't matter that I understood their frustrations or that some part of me even agreed with them. Hearing the doubt in their voices—*their doubt in me*—was like having skin carved away piece by piece.

Could I lead when my own team barely trusted me anymore?

My fingers traced the leather cords of my vambrace absently as I waited in Darrokar's chambers, the faint orange glow of heat crystals reflecting off the volcanic glass walls. The space felt unbearably stifling today, every minute a reminder that I had a million unanswered questions and no sense of where to even begin.

The groan of the chamber doors sliding open made me tense, though the familiar scent that accompanied it eased some of the tautness from my shoulders. Darrokar strode in like a storm contained, wings folding neatly behind him.

"*Luvae,*" he greeted, his deep voice wrapping around me in a comfort it felt almost wrong to accept.

"Darrokar," I replied, straightening where I stood.

I had to start standing up for my people, and that was going to start now. But before I could say anything, he stopped in front of me, holding out a bundle wrapped in dark material. "For you," he said simply.

I blinked, then took it from him carefully. It was heavier than I expected, the texture pliable but sturdy beneath my fingers. A closer look revealed that it wasn't just any material—they were Drakarn warrior leathers. But there were no slits for wings in the back. These were custom.

For a human.

"For me?" I asked, even though the evidence was

staring me in the face. The design wasn't purely Drakarn; it had elements of my Earth uniform woven through it—the reinforced plates, the utilitarian cut meant for ease of motion. More importantly, it was unmistakably mine, from the precise tailoring to the weight beneath the shoulder straps.

Darrokar stepped closer, his golden eyes shimmering. "You cannot fight as one of us if you are not dressed as one of us. Does it not please you?"

I ran my fingers over the intricate detailing along the neckline. "I—no, I mean yes." I shook my head, struggling to find the words. Whatever confidence I'd bolstered before his arrival was unraveling rapidly under his focused attention. "It's perfect."

And nothing I expected.

Before I could muster more than that, Darrokar's claws brushed my hand. It wasn't a gesture I would've noticed before meeting him, but now I couldn't miss it—not the faint scrape of his black scales against my skin, nor the way his touch sent an illicit ripple of something unbearably warm up my arm.

"Let me help you," he said, his voice quieter now, more intimate.

It wasn't a question; it wasn't entirely an order either. My throat tightened as I nodded.

He lifted the armored chest plate, stepping in closer to secure it over my torso. I could feel the heat of him radiating outward even before his claws brushed my sides, buckling a strap here, adjusting a fastening there. There was nothing casual about his movements—they were deliberate and precise.

"You were unhappy when you returned today," he murmured, resting his hands against my shoulders as he adjusted the pauldrons.

I tensed, tilting my head up at him. "How do you—?"

His golden eyes flashed with that knowing look that drove me insane, a faint glimmer of amusement curling at the edge of his mouth. His claws ghosted along my collarbone as he stepped back, admiring his handiwork like a craftsman inspecting their master-piece. "*Luvae,* I see too much to remain ignorant, even when you keep it silent."

"They need better quarters." My voice was sharper than I intended, but I was too raw to smooth it out.

He heard what I wasn't saying. "Whatever mistrust your people hold, it will not endure."

I stared at him, crossing my arms protectively over the newly donned armor. His unwavering confi-dence—his ability to just *decide* something would be fixed—was still something I couldn't entirely reconcile. "They've been locked up for weeks while I've—"

He arched an obsidian brow at that, the smirk softening into something irritatingly tender. "Shall I invite them all here into our bed?"

Our bed.

Aliens didn't seem to exactly be the type for a *define the relationship* talk, but everything Darrokar did, everything he said, let me know that this thing between us wasn't just some passing fascination with the new species in town.

He wanted to keep me.

Without waiting for my response, he moved toward the chamber's exit, inclining his head for me to follow. Despite my lingering doubts, it didn't feel like a request.

The training grounds were blisteringly alive when we arrived, a chaotic melee of roaring warriors, swiping claws, and clashing lavaforged blades.

Darrokar's presence silenced the chaos almost immediately, his warriors bowing their heads briefly in acknowledgment before shifting focus to me.

I could feel their judgment rippling across the space, tinged with curiosity, disdain, and something else I couldn't name.

I stepped closer to Darrokar's side instinctively,

though I regretted letting that self-consciousness fear show a second later. He noticed, of course—his sharp gaze had an infuriating ability to catch things I barely let myself register.

"This is your chance," he said, his voice quiet but firm, pitched low enough for only me to hear. "Do not shy away. Strength does not require familiar words."

Easy for him to say—he had wings, claws, and all the fiery charisma of a walking inferno. I had ... stubbornness and a never-ending list of self-doubts.

"Choose your opponent," he said aloud, this time ensuring every Drakarn present could hear.

The weight of hundreds of eyes turned to me immediately, an almost physical force. I swallowed hard, my heart hammering against the new armor like it, too, didn't trust its protection.

"Her," I said finally, pointing toward a red-scaled, towering warrior standing near the edge of the circle. She was nearly twice my size, her well-toned muscles betraying years of combat experience. If I was going to do this—if I had to *prove* anything—it wouldn't be by taking the easy route.

The arena fell dead silent as we stepped into one of the designated rings. My opponent didn't bother with introductions or a nod—she simply snarled, wings flaring wide as her talons flexed against the blackened stone.

I forced the nerves out of my body, focusing instead on the steadiness of my stance. I wasn't there to die—I was there to learn.

The first blow came swiftly, a wide arc of claws that had more force than calculation behind it. I ducked, twisting my body sharply enough that her wing flap almost pulled me off-balance. Almost.

She didn't give me the chance to recover, lunging forward before I could right myself. Her claws raked downward, and I barely avoided taking the full brunt by pivoting my weight and rolling to the side. The ground beneath my palm burned—a cruel reminder that this wasn't just training. This was the proving ground, and failure wasn't just embarrassing—it was dangerous.

Darrokar stood at the edge of the ring, his presence a dark shadow that drew my awareness despite the chaos of the fight. I didn't need to look to know his eyes were fixed on me, golden and unreadable. Was he watching to see if I could keep up or to see how quickly I'd fall?

Either way, my body moved differently knowing he was there—more desperate to succeed, even as my muscles trembled with the effort.

The warrior snarled again, her claws slashing out at me in a series of calculated strikes, each one driving me back toward the edge of the ring. My feet scrambled against the blackened stone as I blocked her blows with the training blade Darrokar had handed me moments earlier—a blade that suddenly felt absurdly small in my grip.

She wasn't just using brute force anymore; she was toying with me, her attacks designed to keep me defensive and off-balance. I gritted my teeth, frustration simmering with every blow I barely deflected. My breathing was labored, sweat beading on my forehead despite the cool edge of the leathers.

"Is that all you've got, *luvae?*" Darrokar's voice sliced through the tension like the edge of a blade, seemingly mild but deceptively sharp.

I didn't dare look at him, but I could feel the weight of his words. It wasn't mockery—not entirely —but it was enough to provoke the anger simmering just beneath my skin to a boil.

Focusing on my opponent, I lunged forward, feinting to her right before pivoting on my heel and aiming low at her exposed flank. She moved faster than I anticipated—a flash of red scales and the sharp crack of claw against blade as she parried the strike and thrust her wings outward for an additional push.

The force knocked me off-balance, and I stumbled backward, my back perilously close to the molten edge of the ring's boundary.

The crowd of warriors surrounding the arena let out a low, collective rumble—an almost animalistic sound that made me shiver. I couldn't tell if they were impressed or disappointed.

Get it together, Terra.

I swallowed hard and zoomed in on her next move. Her claws lashed out again, and this time, I dropped low before spinning behind her, raising the blade toward her exposed back.

The strike landed.

A shallow cut formed just above her hips— nothing debilitating, but enough to draw a sharp hiss of pain. She flared her wings again, spinning to face me with renewed anger, her stance widening as she prepared to attack.

But I had no intention of waiting.

Before she could regain the advantage, I surged forward, blade poised for another strike. I wasn't foolish enough to think I could overpower her, so I put every ounce of focus into speed and precision, trying to anticipate her reactions.

"Enough."

Darrokar's voice reverberated across the arena, commanding immediate stillness.

My opponent straightened, casting a wary glance toward Darrokar before stepping back and lowering her wings in submission. I didn't know if I imagined the faint smirk tugging at her lips or if it was genuine.

Darrokar strode into the ring with the ease of someone who had never doubted their place in it. His golden eyes met mine, scanning the dirt smeared along my jaw, the faint trembling of my hand where I clutched the hilt of the blade.

"You did not win," he said evenly, his voice firm but lacking malice.

I lifted my chin, willing myself not to flinch beneath the weight of his gaze. "No, but I didn't lose."

His mouth quirked—the barest hint of something that might have been approval. "A draw is not a victory, *luvae*. But it is not a failure either."

One of the warriors behind him chuckled—a low, rumbling sound full of amusement. My cheeks flushed, but Darrokar silenced them with a sharp glance. His authority over them was absolute, even when it appeared effortless.

"You rely too much on your human instincts," he

continued, stepping closer until the scent of smoke and molten stone curled between us. His wings cast a wide, imposing shadow that swallowed the flickering light of the arena's veins. "Speed is not your only weapon, but neither can you abandon it entirely."

I gritted my teeth. I could feel my pride aching under the weight of his critique, but I nodded curtly. "Then teach me."

The mutter of murmurs that rippled through the gathered warriors at my words was barely audible, but I caught it. Those closest to the ring exchanged glances, their pupils narrowing into slits, revealing too much interest in the exchange.

The air between us crackled, thick with implications neither of us fully wanted to voice.

Darrokar stepped closer again, his clawed hand reaching out to turn the hilt of the blade in my grasp just slightly. His touch wasn't rough—more curious, as though he were examining a fragment of a puzzle. "You harbor a fire," he murmured, his gaze slipping back up to meet mine. "But you suffocate it out of fear it will burn too brightly."

"I don't have the luxury," I replied, the words leaving my mouth before I could stop them.

"Nor did I," he said, so quietly it nearly went unheard over the faint hiss of molten stone.

It wasn't the response I had expected, not from him. For just a moment, the walls that so often surrounded him cracked, and something raw and unguarded slipped through.

I should have stepped back—I should have said something, done *something* to break the spell that suddenly bound the air between us. But I didn't.

Instead, I held his gaze. And something in me wondered if, maybe, the thing that bound us wasn't a chain at all.

"Tomorrow," Darrokar said at last, his voice once again the commanding rumble I'd come to recognize. "You will return here. The training will be harder."

I straightened, forcing a smile to mask the exhaustion already settling over me. "I'd be disappointed if it wasn't."

His lips curved just faintly. "Good."

"Ouch, ouch, ouch." My mate limped into our quarters, careful to put her training sword on the hook where it belonged before she collapsed down onto the chaise, dust from the training field blanketing the silk pillows.

She carried herself well on the battlefield. Shalyn was one of the toughest warriors in her training group, and Terra had held her own.

Her red hair, bound in a braid for training, had long ago started unraveling, and now her curls fanned out behind her head like blood upon the rock of our world.

She looked magnificent.

"I'm going to be sore tomorrow," she groaned, rubbing her legs.

"You look sore now." I leaned back in the tub, the warm water steaming around me. "Come soak. Soothe your muscles."

"I think you have ulterior motives." She grinned, stripping off her chest protector. Her silken under-shirt clung to her sweat-slicked body.

"Maybe." I grinned, my fangs flashing. "Or maybe I want to take care of you after such a brutal beating."

She laughed, dropping her pants and kicking them aside. "Brutal? I held my own."

"That you did. Don't sully the water with your filthy clothes." I watched her undress, admiring her curves, her strength, her determination. She was unlike any other female I had ever met.

"You deserved that." She gave me a pointed look.

Perhaps I did. I wouldn't admit it.

She slid into the tub, settling between my legs and leaning back against my chest. I wrapped my arms around her waist, pulling her close. "Better?"

"Much." She sighed, relaxing against me. "I haven't trained like that in ages. Not since before we left Earth."

"We'll make a warrior of you yet." I nuzzled her neck, inhaling her scent. It was stronger than usual, making my tongue tingle. "Why did you leave? Where were you going?" She'd told me of her home, this Earth, but it still sounded unreal to my ears.

"To make a new life. Ours wasn't the only ship to leave. There's been so much discovery, so many planets just waiting for us. The settlement company said we'd all have plenty of space, ample opportunities ... Saying it now, it sounds like a con. I don't know if it was just the te—," she cleared her throat, "the team with me that crashed or if the whole ship came down. There were thousands of people. Do you think we're the only survivors?"

I hadn't lured my mate into the pool to make her morose. I pulled her close. "I'll send out scouts. If there's news of other ships, we'll find them."

She twisted, looking up at me. "You would do that? Why?"

"Because you are my mate." It was simple, instinctual.

"But we barely know each other." She frowned, her brows furrowing.

"I know enough. You are strong and determined. Loyal. Brave. You fight with honor and skill, and you have a fire inside you that burns bright." I let my claws trail over her stomach until she shivered under my touch. "Let me show you."

She turned in my arms, straddling me. Her

breasts pressed against my chest, her nipples hardening against my scales. "I tell you how sore I am from training, and you want to fuck?"

I might have thought she was serious if not for the glint in her eye. "Yes. I want to fuck you." I growled, nipping her bottom lip. "I want to taste you, to fill you, to mark you as mine."

"Then what are you waiting for?" She wrapped her arms around my neck and kissed me. Her lips were soft, her mouth warm, and her tongue eager. She tasted of sweet spices and something else that made my cock throb.

I groaned, pulling her close and deepening the kiss. She arched into me, grinding against my hard length.

I broke away, trailing my mouth down her neck and sucking on her pulse point. "Tell me you're mine."

She shuddered, her fingers digging into my shoulders. "Yours."

I pinned her to the side of the tub. Water splashed around us, hot and steamy. She gazed up at me, her green eyes shining with desire.

My mouth claimed hers again, drinking in her sweet essence as my hands roamed her body, relearning every curve and dip. Her skin was warm and slick from the water, waiting for my exploration. I deepened the kiss, my tongue diving in to dance with hers.

She moaned, arching against me, her nails raking down my back.

I trailed kisses along her jawline, her neck, her collarbone, tasting the salt of her sweat and the unique flavor that was Terra. Her heartbeat pulsed against my tongue as I licked her skin, each beat an echo of her life force. I growled low in my throat.

My fangs throbbed with the need to mark her, to claim her fully as my mate.

"Darrokar," she gasped, her voice husky with desire. "Please, I need you."

Her words were my undoing. I hefted her up onto the edge of the pool and spread her legs.

She trembled as I settled between them, my broad shoulders and wings pushing her thighs wider. She was exposed, open, and utterly vulnerable to me. I felt a surge of possession, my mate bared for my pleasure. Her scent filled my nostrils, musky and sweet, driving me wild.

I traced the sensitive flesh of her inner thigh with the sharp tips of my fangs, a low rumble building in my chest. She shuddered, her fingers spearing through my hair, urging me closer. I chuckled, and the vibrations sent gooseflesh rippling across her skin.

"I need your mouth." Her voice was ragged with desire.

I trailed my tongue along her seam, a line of fire in its wake. She gasped, her hips lifting to meet me. Her folds were slick with arousal; her taste made my cock ache. I delved deeper, my tongue exploring every fold, every sensitive inch of her.

She was swollen, a hard little pearl begging for attention. I lavished it with my tongue, circling the sensitive bud, sucking gently until she was writhing beneath me. The heat of her pressed against my tongue, her hips grinding against my face as I devoured her.

"Darrokar," she moaned, her voice echoing through the chamber, a symphony of pleasure and need.

My name on her lips fanned the flames of my desire, each syllable pushing me closer to the edge.

I growled against her, the vibrations sending shockwaves through her core. My tongue plunged into her, mimicking the thrusts I longed to give her with my cock. She was close, her inner walls clenching around me, her breath coming in short, sharp gasps.

I pulled back, leaving her panting and desperate. She whimpered, her fingers tangling in my hair, trying to pull me back. But I had other plans. I wanted to savor this moment, to draw out her pleasure and my own.

I looked up at her. Her lids were heavy, her pupils dilated, cheeks flushed with desire and exertion. She was a breathtaking sight—my mate, laid bare and eager before me. The air was thick with the scent of her arousal and the steam from the tub, creating an intoxicating atmosphere that only amplified my hunger for her.

"Darrokar, please," she begged, her voice shattered from her need.

A slow, sensual smile curved my lips. "Patience, *luvae*," I murmured, my thumbs tracing idle patterns on her inner thighs.

With deliberate slowness, I reached for the flask of oil resting on the tub's edge. The dark glass glowed with the heat of our world. I poured the oil into my palms, watching as it shimmered in the dim light, reflecting the dance of flames from the heat crystals around us.

The warmth radiated from my hands as I massaged the oil into her skin, starting at her ankles and working my way up her calves, her knees, her thighs. With my claws, I had to be careful, and for the first time in my life, I envied the servants who filed theirs down to nothing but nubs.

Each touch elicited a shiver, a gasp, a soft moan from her lips. Her muscles tensed beneath my fingers, her legs quivering with anticipation as I neared her core.

Once I reached her inner thighs, I paused, the pads of my thumbs dancing along the sensitive flesh just inches from her sex. She writhed, her hips lifting in a silent plea. But I held back, maintaining a steady rhythm that kept her teetering on the edge but never pushing her over.

"You're torturing me," she panted, her hands fisting beneath her.

A dark chuckle rumbled in my chest. "Do you want me to stop, *luvae?*"

Her eyes flashed with defiance, but her body betrayed her, arching into my hands, seeking more contact. "Don't you dare."

A bolt of desire shot through me.

With my claws in the way, I couldn't dip my fingers inside, couldn't spread her open. But I was a Drakarn and would not be so easily cowed. My tail flicked up and teased her entrance, the thick, muscled limb pressing against her slick heat. Her body reacted, clenching around the mere suggestion of penetration.

I smoothed my tail along her folds, coating it with her arousal before pressing forward. The first push of my tail inside was a delicious stretch, her inner walls unyielding but creamy with need. I withdrew, a low growl rumbling in my chest at the sight of her pink, core flesh glistening.

"Darrokar, please," she begged, her hips jerking in a futile attempt to impale herself on my tail.

I captured her mouth in a searing kiss, claiming her moans and whimpers as our tongues tangled. My tail delved deeper, filling her to the hilt, and she screamed into my mouth. Her muscles rippled and clenched around me, milking the sensitive scales.

My cock throbbed. My tail was normally a weapon of war, not pleasure, but the things her body was doing to me sent pulses of desire straight through me.

I withdrew, then plunged back in, a rhythm as relentless as the twin suns. Each thrust dragged a guttural moan from her throat, each withdrawal leaving her crying for me to return. I varied my pace, stoking the flames of her desire, teasing her to the brink then backing off, determined to prolong this delicious torture. Her internal stimulations were adding an extra layer of connection and enjoyment—the pulsing of her heart, the subtle rhythms of her breathing, the heady taste of her pleasure all added to the sensory delight.

"You're so deep," she gasped, her hips bucking wildly, trying to take me as deep as possible. "I need more."

I grinned against her mouth. "Patience, little warrior. I have only just begun."

I adjusted my grip, using my claws to fondle and tease her breasts alongside the relentless thrusts of my tail. I loved the way her nipples hardened into points, begging for attention as she writhed beneath me. My own cock throbbed in time with my pulse, aching to be buried inside her, to fill her completely. But this, this was about her pleasure, about claiming her as mine, body and soul.

"Don't tease me anymore," she pleaded, her voice breaking on a sob. "Please, I need to come."

My response was a deep, rumbling growl and a flex of my tail inside her. That growl turned into a snarl as I finally relented, my tail moving in a wild, frantic rhythm, slamming into her with abandon. Her scream ripped through the chamber as her orgasm crashed over her, her inner walls clamping down on me like a vise. I could feel every pulse, every spasm, her body milking my length for all it was worth.

The sound of her release and the sight of her face contorted in ecstasy pushed me over the edge. I yanked my tail out of her and replaced it with my cock, thrusting like a Drakarn possessed.

I buried myself as deep as possible inside her, my cock throbbing and pulsing as I emptied myself into her waiting body.

We stayed locked together, chest to chest, her legs wrapped around my waist, her breath coming in ragged gasps as we rode out the aftershocks of our passion. My claws held her hips carefully, holding her in place, our hearts thundering against each other.

After what felt like an eternity, I gradually pulled out, my cock glistening with our combined fluids. Terra made an unhappy sound at the loss, her legs falling limp around my waist.

I pulled her back down into the warm water, cradling her against my chest.

I could never have imagined that someone like her would be my mate. But now that I had her, I would fight every force on Volcaryth and anyone from her Earth before I let her go.

FOURTEEN
TERRA

My first thought was *fire.*

Then tornado.

A horn sounded the alarm all through Darrokar's quarters, making my heart pound and jerking him out of a sound sleep beside me.

"What's that? What's going on?" It could have been some sort of drill, but from the tension in Darrokar's form, it was real.

And serious.

"Security has been breached." He scooped up my shirt from where it had fallen on the floor. "Get dressed. Someone will be here soon with a report."

"I need to check on my team." I'd just managed to get them moved to actual rooms in Darrokar's dwelling, though they were all still angry at me for whatever it was I was doing with Darrokar.

Mate.

It was what he called me. It felt right. And if I looked deeper, I might have words of my own I could use, but I was too much of a coward to think too hard about it.

I threw on my shirt and pants quickly, ignoring the lingering soreness from my training the day before. My team—Hawk, Kira, and Vega—might hate me right now, but they were still my responsibility. My people. Whatever was happening, my first priority was making sure they were safe.

Darrokar was already at the door, his broad silhouette framed by the faint orange glow of the crystals embedded in the walls. His golden eyes were hard and focused, slits narrowing as though he were preparing for a battle. When he turned back to face me, there was an edge to his expression that made the air between us feel charged.

Before I could take a step toward the hallway, the door groaned open, and Rath stormed in, his ruby-red scales glinting in the dim light. His wings, half-furled, twitched with tension. He didn't bother with formalities.

"The human, Vega Cross, is missing," he growled, his voice deep and grating.

I froze. "What?"

Darrokar's wings flared, his talons flexing against the stone. "Explain."

"Her quarters were empty when the security check was conducted," Rath said, his gaze flicking briefly to me before locking back on Darrokar. "The guards stationed near her rooms failed to notice her departure. Either she evaded them on foot, or ..." He paused grimly. "Or she was taken."

The words were a punch to the gut. "No," I said immediately, shaking my head. "Vega wouldn't just let herself be taken." And I remembered the conversation we'd had a few days ago. She wanted to escape, to go find the others. Then my mind caught up to the rest of what he said. "Guards? I thought we agreed my people were guests."

I gave Darrokar a pointed look.

"Guests," Darrokar repeated, his voice a low rumble that sent an involuntary shiver down my spine. "Guests do not vanish in the dead of night without explanation." His golden eyes bore into mine, molten and sharp as obsidian, daring me to challenge him further.

"She may have left on her own and then been

taken," Rath suggested, his tail lashing with agitation. "Her trail vanishes abruptly in the crimson deserts. The pattern suggests an aerial attack."

My blood ran cold. If Vega had been taken by air ... "I need to see."

"No." Darrokar's response was immediate, his wings mantling protectively. "The crimson deserts are treacherous enough for those born to them. You will remain here where it's safe."

"Like hell I will." I stepped forward, squaring my shoulders. "Vega is my responsibility. I'm going."

"You do not understand the dangers—"

"Then explain them to me," I cut him off, my voice sharp with frustration. "Because right now, all I see is one of my people missing and you trying to keep me from finding her."

The room crackled with tension. Darrokar's golden eyes blazed, his massive frame seeming to fill the space between us. "The rival clans would consider you a prize beyond measure. My mate, defenseless, different. They would use you to strike at me, at Scalvaris."

"Defenseless? I thought we covered that. I can take care of myself."

"Can you?" He moved closer, his heat radiating against my skin. "Can you fight warriors who have spent their lives perfecting aerial combat? Can you survive the desert's heat storms or navigate the thermal updrafts?"

"No," I admitted, my heart hammering. "But I know Vega. If she left willingly, I might know where she's headed. If she was taken, I can help predict her actions."

Rath shifted uncomfortably, clearly wanting to speak but waiting for Darrokar's response.

Darrokar's jaw clenched, the muscles in his neck tightening. "You know more than you're telling me."

It wasn't a question. I swallowed hard, guilt and necessity warring in my heart. I'd promised to keep the others a secret, but with Vega gone and a group of Drakarn ready to scour the desert to find her, how long could they stay hidden?

"Tell me what you know," my mate demanded.

The accusation hung between us, heavy as molten stone. I met his gaze steadily, even as my heart threatened to beat out of my chest. "I know Vega. I know she's smart, capable, and wouldn't leave without a reason."

"A reason you won't share." His voice was dangerously quiet now, a rumble that seemed to vibrate through my bones.

"It doesn't matter." The words tasted bitter. "Let me help you find her."

Darrokar's tail lashed, his frustration evident in every line of his powerful frame. "You ask me to trust you while you keep secrets that could endanger us all."

"My lord," Rath interrupted, his expression grim. "The longer we delay, the colder the trail grows. If rival clans have her ..."

"Prepare the search party," Darrokar ordered, not taking his eyes off me. "I want our fastest warriors ready to fly within the hour."

Rath nodded sharply and left, the door hissing shut behind him.

As soon as we were alone, Darrokar closed the distance between us. His claws ghosted along my arm, a touch that was both possessive and questioning. "Why do you resist telling me the truth? Do you not trust me to protect your people?"

"Some secrets aren't mine to share." I fought the urge to lean into his touch.

His other hand cupped my face, forcing me to look up at him. "And if those secrets get someone killed? What then, *luvae?*"

The endearment, spoken with such raw emotion,

made my chest ache. "That's why I need to go with you. I can help."

"You could die." His thumb traced my cheekbone. "The desert shows no mercy, and neither do our enemies."

"I'm not asking for mercy." I covered his claws with mine, feeling the rough texture of his scales against my palm. "I'm asking for a chance to protect my own."

Something shifted in his expression—pride mixed with fear, anger with understanding. "You will follow my orders without question. If I tell you to retreat, you retreat. If I tell you to hide, you hide. No arguments."

"Not a one."

I would keep my word. And somehow figure out how to untangle this knot before it ruined everything.

When I found Vega, I was going to *kill* her.

Terra's arms were a vise around my neck, her body a surprising weight pressed against my chest as we knifed through the wind's violent bursts. Below, the crimson sands unspooled, an endless landscape warped by waves of ferocious heat.

The wind, thick with the grit of the wasteland, delivered the faint tang of her—fear, sharp and undeniable, a core of determination, and beneath it, something furtive. Something that tightened the skin around my fangs with gnawing suspicion.

She was hiding something.

A thermal punched at my wings, and I corrected our course automatically, my gaze raking the merciless terrain. The desert was a predator, even to those of my blood. For humans? It was death.

Ten of my fiercest warriors shadowed us, their flight a testament to years of honed discipline. Rath was among them, his ruby scales flashing beneath the brutal sunlight. The volatile temper that usually simmered beneath his surface was notably absent, replaced by a focused intensity I knew intimately.

He, too, was on the hunt.

"There!" Terra's voice, thin but clear, sliced through the wind's roar. Her finger jabbed toward a jagged obsidian spire, a black fang tearing at the horizon. "That rock formation. It's the only shade for miles."

My wings stiffened, a prickle of unease tracing my spine. She was right, a certainty in her tone that scraped against my senses. It spoke of experience, of a familiarity that shouldn't exist. Unless ...

"You know this place." It wasn't a question.

Her body's stillness against mine was an answer in itself. "No, but it's where I'd hide out if I needed to disappear."

The word hung between us, heavy with unspoken implications. From whom? From me?

Banking sharply, I angled towards the spire, a silent command for the others to maintain altitude, circle wide. As we closed the distance, the scent hit me, acrid and unmistakable—Drakarn. A significant number. And beneath that reek, the faint, metallic tang of humans.

Plural.

Involuntarily, my grip around Terra tightened, my talons flexing against her back. She gasped, a sharp intake of breath, but I couldn't force my hold to ease. Every instinct screamed that she knew. Had known all along that more of her kind were out there.

She'd spoken of her ship, of the thousands aboard. Had she truly been ignorant of their fate? Or had even that been a carefully constructed lie?

We landed on a thin ridge, the twisted obsidian shielding us from immediate view. Below, nestled within a natural amphitheater carved by the wind, sprawled a rival clan's encampment. Sentries patrolled the perimeter, their wings held half-spread, struggling against the scorching air. And there, tethered within a sheltered alcove ...

"Six," I growled, the sound a low reverberation in my chest. "There are six more of your kind with your Vega."

Terra's heart hammered against my scales, a frantic drumbeat against my own. She offered no denial, her silence a damning indictment.

"You knew." I released her, the physical act mirroring the desperate need to put space between us. The betrayal burned, sharper and more insidious than any desert sun. "All this time, you knew there were others."

"Darrokar—"

"Don't." My tail lashed, a swift, violent flick that sent a spray of crimson sand arcing through the air. "Did you imagine I wouldn't protect them? That I would ever bring them harm?"

Her green eyes locked onto mine, unwavering, laced with a fierce defiance that offered no apology. "I couldn't risk it. Not with their lives on the line."

Her words struck with the force of a physical blow, leaving me winded. My chest constricted, but it was the dull ache beneath the surge of anger that truly unraveled me. "But you could risk *us*? Risk severing the bond between us? The trust we've bled to build?" My voice dropped, the raw edges of my hurt scraping against the air. "I am your mate, Terra."

"And they're my responsibility." Her tone was clipped, every syllable precise, but a tremor ran beneath the surface. She took a step closer and lifted her hand.

Even as her scent—spiced earth and something uniquely hers, something that burrowed deep—enveloped me, my instincts screamed a warning. I recoiled, a deliberate step back that widened into a full extension of my wings, stirring the dust into a swirling vortex between us. Her hand froze mid-air, a fleeting flicker of something akin to pain crossing her features before her jaw tightened, snapping into that familiar soldier's resolve I both loathed and admired.

"Don't," I repeated, my voice a low, guttural rumble, barely leashed. My wings curved inward for a heartbeat, shielding me in an involuntary gesture before settling against my back. "You lied to me. Do you understand what you've done? Every fiber of my being is designed to protect you, to trust your word as law. You are *mine*."

Her lips parted, but before either of us could plunge deeper into this chasm of fractured trust, a shadow swept over us. I snapped my gaze skyward, recognizing the unmistakable shift of Rath's broad wings, a stark silhouette against the harsh light, signaling movement within the camp below. A brutal reminder that our enemies remained, even as the world between Terra and me felt as though it was imploding.

I turned back to her, my muscles coiled, every nerve ending screaming. The urge to drag her close, to reassure myself of her physical presence, warred violently with the equally powerful need to thrust her away, to create distance. But beneath the consuming anger, the relentless hum of the bond persisted, an invisible tether binding me to her in ways I couldn't sever, even if I desired it.

"Stay here," I commanded, the order sharper than intended. "Those *kervash* won't hesitate to use you against me if they see you."

Her shoulders squared, her entire demeanor coiling like a struck serpent. "I can fight," she spat, each word laced with iron and defiance.

I leaned in close, my words a near-snarl, the raw fury a mask for the agonizing vulnerability she'd exposed. "Do you think I question your strength, Terra? Do you believe me blind to it? But down there, strength alone is insufficient. I will not risk losing you."

Her gaze flickered for a fraction of a heartbeat, a raw, untamed emotion breaching the surface before she ruthlessly suppressed it, drawing down those impenetrable walls she so easily erected.

I wanted to grab her, shake her until the facade crumbled, until she dropped that damnable guard—for once, for me. But Rath's signal flashed again, more urgent now, pulling my attention away before the unspoken could be said. Before I could confess the chilling realization: her betrayal cut so deep not because it revealed weakness, but because it illuminated the terrifying extent to which I had already surrendered my heart.

"That wasn't a suggestion." I spread my wings, the membranes stretching taut, catching the harsh light. "You've proven you can't be trusted. Don't compound your error."

The raw hurt that flashed across her features nearly shattered my resolve. But the lie, however delivered, remained. And now, we plunged into battle with compromised trust and unknown threats.

I launched myself into the air before she could retort, catching a thermal that lifted me higher. Below, the camp stirred, a disturbed nest of vipers. They'd seen us.

Good.

Let them come.

Rath fell into formation beside me, his voice a rumble carried on the wind. "Movement to the east. They're attempting to move the humans."

A snarl tore from my throat, baring my fangs. "Take the others. Cut off their escape route. I'll engage their warriors."

He hesitated, his gaze flicking toward the alcove where the humans were held captive. "If they resist?"

"Subdue. No fatalities." I met his gaze, the

command leaving no room for interpretation. "These humans are under my protection now. All of them."

A sharp nod acknowledged the order. He peeled away, leading the others in a wide arc to intercept the enemy clan attempting to flee with their captives. I tucked my wings, plummeting towards the cluster of rival warriors spilling from their makeshift shelters.

The first Drakarn never registered my approach. My talons ripped across his wing membranes, the tearing sound sickeningly satisfying as he cartwheeled into the sand. The second managed to gain altitude, but a brutal sweep of my tail sent him spiraling back to earth.

More swarmed to meet me, their scales a harsh variety of colors under the blazing sun. They fought with a practiced savagery, but I hadn't earned the title of Warrior Lord of Scalvaris through chance. My claws found the vulnerable gaps between their scales, my wings a blur of motion, deflecting their clumsy attacks.

A flicker of movement at the edge of my vision snagged my attention—Terra, disregarding my direct order and on the move. Fury and a chilling spike of fear warred within me.

The distraction was costly. Claws raked across my shoulder, a searing line of pain drawing blood. I roared, spinning to face my assailant, when Rath's voice, laced with urgency, ripped through the din.

"Darrokar!"

His warning arrived too late. A hulking warrior, his scales the color of a gathering storm, positioned himself above me, preparing a dive that would have shredded my wings. But then, a flash of red hair erupted between us.

Terra.

She'd scaled the treacherous obsidian spire and launched herself at my attacker, her smaller form colliding with his far larger one. They tumbled through the air, a tangled mass of limbs and scales, and for a terrifying heartbeat, I thought she would fall.

But she was a whirlwind of controlled chaos. Using his momentum against him, she twisted, redirecting his descent into the jagged face of the spire. The impact reverberated through the rock, showering us with black glass shards.

I caught her before she hit the ground, the frantic rhythm of my heart slamming against my ribs. "I ordered you to stay back."

"Yeah, well, you're welcome," she shot back, her grip tight on my shoulders, her eyes blazing with adrenaline. "Now put me down. They need help."

They. Always others.

But she was correct. The battle's focus had shifted to where Rath and my warriors were locked in a brutal melee, struggling to shield the humans. I set Terra down behind a fallen boulder, ignoring her immediate protests.

"Stay. Here." My growl was a promise of violence. "Or I'll chain you to it myself."

Her mouth opened in protest, but I was already airborne, my wings slicing through the humid, smoke-tinged air as I hurtled towards the heart of the conflict.

The battlefield was a riot of guttural snarls, desperate shouts, and the brutal clash of honed steel against obsidian-hard claws. Rath stood as a bulwark between the cluster of humans and the relentless assault, his massive crimson form a living shield. But his stance was off—his weight unevenly distributed, his wings trembling with subtle, unnatural spasms. His gaze kept flicking towards one human woman, her face pale but resolute, clutching a makeshift weapon with surprising ferocity.

I banked low, the rush of displaced air churning grit and blood-soaked sand as I targeted the largest of the remaining rival Drakarn. His scales were a dull, mottled gray and covered in scars, a testament to countless battles. He raised a jagged blade, poised to strike down a fallen warrior who lay clutching his wounded side, blood blooming in the sand beneath him.

The subtle tightening of the air, the near-silent intake of breath from the human woman—her eyes wide with horror—told me she saw it too. I could almost hear her gasp as my talons raked across the enforcer's back, sending a shower of blood and splintered goethite scales flying. He roared in pain and fury as his weapon spun from his grasp, landing with a muffled thud in the sand-soaked ground.

His head snapped towards me as I landed heavily, my wings flaring for balance, the impact jarring my legs. My fighters roared their approval, the sight of their Warrior Lord bolstering their resolve.

The enforcer staggered to his feet, his back a ruin, his movements sluggish. He lunged, more out of desperation than skill. It didn't matter. I sidestepped with a fluid grace, my tail whipping around, catching him mid-charge. Bone crunched against bone, a sickening sound, and he was airborne for a fleeting moment before slamming into a jagged outcrop. He didn't rise. The fight drained from his eyes, leaving them vacant.

The tide of the battle shifted. I tracked Rath's

movements, a brief assessment of his position and the threat he posed. More of the humans were upright than I'd anticipated, their crude weapons wielded with a surprising amount of fierce determination.

Whatever fear or burning anger fueled them, it bought the precious seconds my warriors needed to gain the upper hand.

My focus snapped back to the remaining rival Drakarn, their attempts to regroup failing miserably. Their scattered formation reeked of panic; their leader was either dead or had fled.

Fools.

I surged forward again, claws crunching on fragments of scale and bone as I slammed into another straggler. His yelp was abruptly cut short beneath my weight, the air expelled from his lungs as I drove him into the sand. His body convulsed once, then went still. A feral snarl tightened my lips, though I suppressed the surge of satisfaction. Such indulgence was a waste of energy, a luxury I couldn't afford.

"Press the attack! Leave no survivors!" I bellowed, my voice a weapon that cut through the chaos. The commanding tone galvanized my warriors. Discipline, precision, overwhelming force —it yielded the same brutal efficiency as always.

The rival Drakarn faltered, their resistance fracturing. Instincts for self-preservation eclipsed any semblance of strategy.

Their retreat was a disorganized rout. My warriors pursued relentlessly, each strike precise, aimed to incapacitate or kill. The sands drank deeply of fresh blood, the air thick with the metallic tang and the acrid smell of scorched flesh. The wounded were abandoned, left to writhe in pools of their own lifeblood under the pitiless suns. A grimly familiar sight.

The battle's frenzy subsided, leaving an echoing silence. The heady scent of victory, usually exhilarating, left a bitter taste on my tongue. I planted my claws firmly, wings folding against my back as I surveyed the remnants of the carnage.

My gaze snagged on Rath. He stood unmoving, his bulk still shielding the huddled humans. His breathing was ragged, a low, rhythmic rasp against the backdrop of fading battle cries.

I landed beside the alcove, the humans shrinking back, their faces etched with fear and a fragile defiance. Vega stood at the forefront, her posture protective despite her obvious exhaustion.

She inclined her head, a subtle gesture of acknowledgement. Her gaze swept over the fallen

Drakarn. "This didn't exactly go as planned. Some asshole grabbed me as soon as I left the city."

"You speak our words." Was this another human trick?

Vega shrugged. "I'm a quick study."

I had to leave it aside for now. "Terra is unharmed." I glanced over my shoulder, seeing my mate approaching, disregarding my earlier command.

Of course.

The two women exchanged a brief, assessing look, a silent communication passing between them. I recognized the subtle narrowing of Terra's eyes, the telltale sign she was calculating which truths to reveal.

Rath approached, his wings held tight against his back. "The area is secure."

I studied the humans, noting their reactions. One in particular drew my attention—a slight female with vibrant purple hair who couldn't seem to tear her gaze away from Rath. That was a problem for later.

"We return to Scalvaris," I announced, spreading my wings, my shadow falling across them. "All of us. Arrangements will be made for these women."

If my mate had any objection, she kept it to herself.

The flight back was taut with unspoken tensions, the air thick with simmering emotions and unasked questions. Terra rode with me again, but the familiar warmth of her was absent, replaced by a rigid stiffness that felt like a physical wound.

I watched my warriors pair off with the rescued humans, noting the careful way Rath positioned himself to carry the purple-haired female to the medical cavern.

The twin suns disappeared as we descended into Scalvaris. I landed on my private balcony, setting Terra down with a force harder than intended.

She stumbled, catching herself, her green eyes meeting mine. They held a turbulent mix of defiance and something I couldn't decipher. Regret? Fear? The clarity I once possessed was gone.

Only one question mattered, the one that had clawed at me since the battle had begun. My voice was stripped bare, raw with need in the fading light.

"Will you ever trust me?"

Oh god, I'd fucked up. Big time.

My hands were still shaky from the less-than-smooth flights to and from that dust-choked excuse for a hideout. Darrokar's gaze felt like a physical blow, and honestly? I deserved every ounce of the accusation radiating off him.

Instinct screamed I should've laid everything bare from the start, trusted him, consequences be damned. But the *others*. I couldn't ignore the responsibility I had to them.

The steady rhythm of the underground river in the distance did nothing to slow the frantic hammering of my pulse. Darrokar remained a towering silhouette against the soft glow of heat crystals embedded in the walls. Every line of his body screamed tension, his golden eyes, those vertical slits, burning twin holes right through me.

Words were inadequate, clumsy shields against the raw emotion crackling between us.

"Why?" The weight of his question settled on my chest, heavy and suffocating. "You lied. About everything."

"Not everything," I managed, my voice low, strained. It sounded weak, even to my own ears. My hands betrayed my inner turmoil as my thumbs rubbed agitated circles against the worn fabric of my borrowed pants. "When we woke up ... it was chaos. They're mostly civilians, Darrokar. My job is to protect them. When we saw you, your warriors coming for us ... I told Selene and Lexa to hide them. We couldn't risk—" My voice hitched, the lie sticking in my throat like grit.

"Couldn't risk what?" He loomed, his sheer size filling my vision, stealing the air from my lungs. "Risk trusting me?"

"Yes." The word burst out, sharper than intended, the blunt admission tasting like ash.

His wings flared, the membranes shifting, and I saw the subtle flex of the claws at his sides. But I pushed on, the need to explain, however poorly, eclipsing my worry.

"Yes, I couldn't risk trusting you *yet*. You don't understand what it was like. We went to sleep on a ship, expecting ... Earth. We woke up to *this*. Fucking sand lizards attacked us before some of us were even fully out of the cryo-pods. This whole damn planet has tried to kill us since we opened our eyes. How could I trust *anything*?"

The crystalline light in the room did nothing to soften the harsh planes of his face, the molten fury still simmering in his gaze. That anger wasn't foreign —some emotions transcended galaxies. But this was different. This wasn't directed at some faceless enemy; this was aimed squarely at *me*.

"That might hold if we were speaking of the first days," he said finally, his voice dangerously soft, the quiet menace more cutting than any roar. "But you thought I would allow them ... allow *you* ... to suffer within my city? Despite every breath within me screaming to protect you?"

Guilt twisted in my gut, a sharp, sickening lurch. "That wasn't my intention."

"Then clarify it for me, *luvae*." He stalked closer, until there was barely a breath between us, trapping me in the inferno of his gaze. "Tell me why you withheld the truth."

The room felt smaller. I needed a moment, a

breath, to gather the scattered pieces of my rationale. "I didn't ..." My breath hitched as I met his unwavering gaze, the raw hurt there a far sharper torment than any outward rage. "I do trust you. I *wanted* to trust you. But they were my responsibility."

His expression didn't soften, but something behind the gold flickered, a flicker of ... understanding? "And now?"

"Now?" I blew out a frustrated breath, the sound ragged. "Now, I don't know what the hell I'm doing anymore." I pressed two fingers hard against my temple, the gesture more forceful than necessary. "My head and my heart are a damn mess because of you."

"You speak as if it is a curse," he murmured, though the underlying tension in his voice hadn't fully dissipated. His golden eyes narrowed, dissecting my defenses like a surgeon's blade.

"Because it feels like one," I admitted, the words leaving a bitter taste. "Because I'm terrified of trusting it. Of trusting *you*."

His wings lifted slightly, the movement subtle but significant, eclipsing the faint light filtering from a high crevice, making him seem impossibly vast, impossibly *other*.

Because he is, that traitorous voice whispered in

my mind, the one I'd ruthlessly silenced with every lie, every deflection, every self-deceptive argument that this connection couldn't possibly be as profound as it felt.

"And yet," he said, his voice dropping, becoming a low thrum that vibrated through me, "you do."

My breath hitched. His proximity was overwhelming, too close, yet utterly necessary, a grounding force in the swirling chaos of my emotions. I didn't understand it, not completely. But I was beginning to understand *us*, and that realization was more terrifying than any alien predator.

"I ..." The words caught, snagged by a sudden surge of panic, my pride a stubborn knot in my throat. I couldn't articulate it, couldn't give voice to the gaping void inside me that only his presence seemed to fill. But my body betrayed me, a subtle shift bringing me closer, erasing the inches between us until I could feel the radiating heat of his scales against my skin, his scent, that intoxicating mix of spice and something uniquely Darrokar, engulfing me.

"Tell me," he commanded softly, the word a quiet insistence, not a roared demand. It was a steady anchor in the storm raging within me. "Do you love me?"

Every muscle locked tight.

The question, stripped bare of any artifice, hit with brutal force. My towering, formidable Warrior Lord, demanding nothing less than the unvarnished truth of my heart—a truth I'd barely dared to whisper to myself.

"I don't know how to do this," I breathed, the confession barely audible, trembling in the charged air. "I've been trained for a thousand things, Darrokar. But not this. Not *you*."

"That is not an answer, *luvae*." His voice deepened, becoming impossibly intimate, laced with a raw thread I couldn't quite decipher—hope, perhaps, though he guarded it fiercely.

I could have lied. Deflected. Offered some carefully crafted response to sidestep the core of his question. But the desire to shield myself, to maintain that brittle control, had fractured.

The realization struck with sudden, undeniable force, the words tumbling out like a dam had broken. "I love you." The admission was a raw whisper, choked with the unfamiliar burn of unshed tears prickling at the back of my eyes. It was a fragile offering, terrified and utterly sincere. "I'm so sorry. I—"

His large, clawed hands cupped my face, the

unexpected gentleness of his touch in contrast to his imposing strength. My words faltered, dying the moment his golden gaze locked onto mine, holding me captive. My chest rose and fell too quickly, my heart a frantic drum against the deafening silence stretching between us, but his touch remained steady, anchoring.

"You are my mate," he breathed, the words a fierce whisper, quieter than I'd ever heard him, but undeniably powerful. His thumbs brushed over my cheeks, a subtle caress erasing the tears I hadn't even realized were falling. "That means I have already forgiven you."

"But I—"

"You are mine, Terra," he stated, his voice still soft, but edged with steel. "Always. There is nothing to forgive."

And before I could argue, before I could even think to resist—as if resistance was a possibility I truly entertained—his lips claimed mine.

His kiss was firm, insistent, and imbued with a surprising tenderness. I met his urgency, my hands fisting in the rough fabric of his tunic, fighting the instinctive urge to drag him closer, to meld our bodies into one. The quiet intensity of the moment was overwhelming, a raw vulnerability that compelled me to pull away and to hold on tighter all at the same time.

His tongue slipped past my lips, a silent invitation that I accepted without hesitation. The taste of him was intoxicating, a heady mix of something uniquely his and the lingering heat of the Volcaryth suns. A shiver danced down my spine, and I pressed closer, the solid warmth of his body an anchor.

His hands moved from my face, one tracing the curve of my back, pressing me against him, the other cupping the nape of my neck, tilting my head to deepen the kiss. I felt the subtle scrape of his claws against my skin, a reminder of the untamed power he held, even in this tender embrace.

Fear should have been my first reaction, but all I felt was a surge of excitement, a thrill that chased away the lingering shadows of guilt and doubt.

A low growl rumbled in his chest, against my mouth, sending a delicious tremor through me, a silent challenge I had no desire to refuse. My heart hammered, a frantic rhythm echoing the possessive urgency of his kiss. My fingers tightened in his tunic, pulling him closer, unwilling to cede even a millimeter of space.

He broke the kiss, just long enough for his gaze to lock with mine. His pupils were dilated, the gold of his irises burning with an intensity that stole my breath. "You are mine, Terra," he murmured, his voice a rough caress.

"Yes. Yours." The words were out before I consciously formed them, a raw response that earned me a fierce, possessive smile, a flash of predatory satisfaction that sent a fresh wave of shivers down my spine. His wings shifted behind him, the leathery whisper of their movement filling the brief silence before he lowered his head to kiss me again.

My hands, freed from their grip on his tunic, traced the hard line of his chest, feeling the thick muscles beneath the fabric. He tensed subtly as my fingers brushed over a scar, deeper than the others, his claws at the small of my back twitching almost imperceptibly. I paused, my fingertips tracing the uneven edges of the faded mark. "What's this from?" I murmured, pulling back slightly to meet his gaze.

He hesitated, his eyes flicking away for second before returning to mine. "A long time ago," he began, his voice suddenly thick with the weight of buried memories. "When I was young. Foolish. I underestimated an opponent." He shrugged, a dismissive gesture that didn't quite reach his eyes. "A lesson learned in blood and pain." His hand covered mine, pressing my palm firmly against his chest. "It does not matter now."

Before I could question further, he swept me off my feet, my legs wrapping around his hips just below the curve of his wings as he stalked towards the sleeping platform. My clothing seemed to vanish in a flurry of frantic movement, impatient hands stripping away the barriers until it was skin against heated scale.

He laid me on the soft silks of the platform, his gaze never leaving mine as he loomed above me, a magnificent predator claiming his prize. His body was a breathtaking blend of muscle and sharp angles, the obsidian scales gleaming in the gentle light filtering through the crystalline formations, and a surge of lust pulsed through me.

This formidable creature, this alien warrior, was mine, and I devoured him with my eyes, tracing the powerful lines of his wings, the intricate patterns of his scales. His golden eyes burned into me, reflecting a raw, possessive intensity that mirrored my own desire.

"You're beautiful," I whispered, the words barely audible, yet they seemed to echo in the stillness of the cavern. His wings flared at the simple declaration.

His lips curved into a slow, predatory smile that sent a shiver of anticipation down my spine. "So are you, *luvae*." His voice was a low purr, a vibration against my skin that ignited a firestorm within me. He leaned down, his wings partially unfurling, enveloping us in a private cocoon of shadow and heat. "I want to hear you say it again," he murmured against my lips, his breath warm and heavy.

My heart pounded against my ribs, my stomach flipping with a potent cocktail of anticipation and nervous excitement. I felt exposed, vulnerable, yet the familiar tremor of fear was absent, replaced by an overwhelming sense of rightness. "I love you, Darrokar."

A growl rumbled in his chest, a sound of pure pleasure and possession as his lips claimed mine again, the kiss fierce, demanding, leaving no doubt of his claim. His mouth moved to the sensitive skin of my neck, his tongue tracing a tantalizing path, sending shivers cascading down my spine. The subtle scratch of his fangs against my flesh was a thrilling reminder of the predator lurking beneath the surface, and I shuddered, my nails digging into the solid muscle of his back, urging him closer.

"More," I gasped, my voice a breathy plea, and it was enough.

He pulled back, his gaze burning into mine, his lips curled into a wickedly seductive smile. "Anything for you, *luvae*."

My hips arched instinctively, my body begging for the contact only he could provide. A deep laugh vibrated through his chest as he shifted, his movements fluid and deliberate. In one swift motion, he rolled us over, pinning me beneath him, his weight a welcome pressure.

His cock, thick and pulsing with anticipation, pressed against my entrance, and a sharp gasp escaped my lips as he slowly, deliberately, pushed inside me. It was everything I remembered, every time before, only amplified, the molten heat of him filling me, stretching me in ways I hadn't thought possible.

He moved slowly at first, his hips grinding against mine in a wild rhythm. I urged him deeper, wanting to lose myself completely within him. He obliged with a low growl, his cock throbbing inside me, each pulse sending shockwaves of pleasure through my core. The sensation was almost too intense, the raw heat of him, the satisfying stretch, the profound sense of being utterly consumed. I arched my back, pressing my breasts against his scaled chest, and he groaned, the sharp tips of his fangs grazing my neck.

"Darrokar," I gasped, my voice a ragged whisper, but he offered no verbal response, only a deeper growl as his hips began to move faster, driving into me with a dark, relentless intensity that left me breathless and trembling beneath him.

His pace quickened, each thrust hitting that elusive sweet spot deep within me, blurring my vision, silencing the frantic chatter of my mind. I clung to him, my nails digging into the unyielding strength of his scales as I met his every movement, my hips rising to take him even deeper, craving the exquisite friction.

The air thickened with the sound of our ragged breathing, the slick slap of skin against scale, and the low, guttural sounds of pleasure that escaped his lips with each powerful thrust.

I felt the coil of pleasure building within me, tightening, intensifying with each pass of his cock, until it was a living thing, humming with unbearable tension just beneath my skin. His lips found mine again, the kiss fierce, possessive, a primal claiming that left no room for doubt. I met his urgency with equal fervor, my body moving in perfect sync with his, meeting every thrust with a desperate hunger that bordered on madness.

The coil inside me snapped, and a cry tore from my throat, swallowed by the intensity of his kiss. My inner muscles clenched around him, milking his cock as wave after wave of mind-shattering pleasure crashed over me, pulling me under. He groaned, his hips stuttering, his movements becoming ragged as he followed me over the precipice, his seed pulsing into me in hot, rhythmic bursts. We clung to each other, our bodies slick with sweat, trembling with the aftershocks of our shared climax, the heat of our skin melded together, our hearts hammering in unison.

The silence that followed was profound, grounding. I lay nestled against him, the steady rise and fall of his chest beneath my cheek a reassuring anchor—breathing, alive, *real*. My fingers traced the warmth of his scaled abdomen absently, the soft glow from the crystal formations painting us in flickering firelight.

Darrokar's arm lay possessively across my waist, his long tail draped loosely over the edge of the platform. His warmth enveloped me, and for a fleeting, precious moment, the restless storm in my mind finally quieted.

"I've spent my whole life trying to do everything

on my own," I said quietly, the words a soft crack in the stillness. His claws, tracing lazy patterns on my arm, paused briefly.

"You do not have to anymore." His voice was low, molten with a certainty that resonated deep within me, stealing my breath.

"I'm scared," I whispered, pressing my forehead against his chest, unsure if I wanted him to acknowledge the vulnerability or pretend he hadn't heard. Admitting fear was a luxury I rarely afforded myself —not openly, not even internally. But there, cocooned in his warmth, the words spilled out, unchecked. "Scared of what I'll become if I let this ... let *us* ... take me. I'm afraid of losing control."

His wing shifted then, wrapping around me like a shield, and his lips brushed against my temple, the lingering warmth sending a wave of sensation rippling through me. The cavern air smelled of heat, of sweat, of him—so distinctly Drakarn, so undeniably Darrokar.

"You will not lose yourself," he murmured, his voice fierce yet achingly gentle, as if I were as fragile as I was flawed. "If you are afraid, then I will carry that fear as my own, just as I will carry any burden that challenges you. Your strength is your own, Terra, but it belongs to me now as well."

Something wrenched in my chest then, not the sharp sting of shame or the friction of anger, but a quiet shift, a slow surrender. A gradual loosening of tension I hadn't even realized I'd been carrying.

I didn't respond, the sudden weight of his words a heavy lump in my throat. But I felt his hand tighten against my back, his warmth a tangible reassurance that he wasn't going anywhere, and the frantic rhythm of my pulse began to slow. Quietly, perhaps with more desperation than I intended, I pressed my fingers against his warm abdomen and closed my eyes.

This place, this life, wasn't the plan. But I'd take the alien beside me over any plan I'd ever imagined.

And I'd thank fate every night I slept in his arms.

The burning in my chest felt like I'd swallowed a piece of the lava that runs through this cursed planet. It wasn't the ache of a battle wound, or the sharp stab of betrayal. No, this was different.

Fucked up, even by my standards.

It clawed, not at my flesh, but at the very core of me, a hollow ache that echoed, a desperate need that whispered, *her*.

I could still taste the subtle sweetness in the air, faint but undeniable. The scent I had caught in the battle against those damned *kervash*, now tinged with something else.

It wasn't just a scent. It was an invasion that was tearing through my carefully constructed wall of self-control. My internal fires seemed to burn hotter, threatening to set my ruby scales ablaze. I had left, stomped through protocol and practically begged information from healers like a fledgling but got nothing. Then I'd snarled and still got nothing, but she was there.

I knew it in my blood.

My claws scraped against the stone walls as I pushed open the oversized door of the healer's cavern. It was always too bright in there, the heat crystals pulsating an irritating light that made my scales itch. The scent of crushed herbs and scented oils filled my nostrils, a sickly sweet smell that normally did nothing, but now, it was layered with something else, *her* scent that I had tracked through the air, even faint.

My wings twitched with an energy I couldn't place—part anticipation, part rage at the waiting.

"Rath!" The sharp voice of the Mysha cut through the thick air. Her golden scales flickered as she turned, her yellow slit pupils narrowed in annoyance. She was old, ancient even, her voice edged with an authority that only age and skill could grant. Most of my warriors flinched under her gaze.

Even I felt a prickle of unease.

"What in the twin suns do you think you're doing? This is a place of healing, not the war council." Her tone was clipped, practical. She never failed to remind me I was a walking, breathing inferno.

"I need to see the humans." My tone was low, a rumble in my chest. My need to get closer to *her* burned so hot that I only managed to maintain a modicum of civility.

She huffed, a sound like pressurized steam venting. "For what purpose? They are all various levels of heat sick and need to recover."

"It's important. Council business." I was on the war council. It was my business. A technical truth, but the words felt like lies. "One of them had purple in her hair."

Mysha's head tilted back, amusement flickered inside her dark eyes, as though I had just told a rather poor joke. "They are half-dead from the heat and covered in enough dust and sand to choke a *dranith*." She gestured with a clawed hand towards the rows of beds carved into the rock walls, each occupied by a listless human. "None of them is in any shape to speak to the council. They are being medically contained."

My claws tightened. I wanted to roar my frustration, to demand she bring *her* forth now. But I held back. Her dismissal stoked the fires in my chest, a constant burning that threatened to burst out, not that she would care. "I shall decide whether she can speak."

"You will not. Leave, go back to the training grounds, and work your rage out." Her voice was firm, absolute. "You disturb the healing." She waved her hand as if swatting away an insect.

I fought to contain the roaring in my ears. My wings pushed against the confines of the cavern walls, restless, itching for flight. It was there, faint but unmistakable. Mixed with the sickly herbs and oils, I caught a trace, her aroma. Like a desert flower, sweet, delicate, but with a hint of something wild underneath ... *mine*.

It twisted inside me, an undeniable, visceral pull. It clawed at my throat and settled in my stomach, both painful and enticing, the promise of something more.

I took a step toward the beds, my gaze sweeping over figures hidden under white sheets and only the occasional limb visible, looking for a specific face and scent combination. The scent grew stronger as I moved closer, a magnetic pull. I wanted to touch, to inhale, to press my nose to her skin and confirm what my body told me was true. My fangs tingled, a sensation that ignited a deeper fire inside me, an urge I'd never truly expected to feel.

"Leave this place, Fire Heart." Her yellow eyes could see my intentions, piercing through my attempts at discretion with a knowing sharpness that bordered on irritation. "I will not let you disturb these patients."

I balled my fist, claws digging into my palm. "You cannot deny me this, elder; I have a *right*." The words hissed past my teeth.

"Your right ends where your tantrums begin." She glared with a look that could burn an entire forest. "If you continue this nonsense, I will summon the guards to escort you out. Consider yourself warned."

I knew from her tone the threat wasn't idle. She would make good on her word. And I still couldn't see. I took a deep breath. It was not worth an all-out battle. I had to be smart. Patient. She was my mate. If the bond was what I felt, then she was more important than anything. "Fine," I ground out, "but I'll be back."

Once in the open air, I finally felt the flames inside me simmering down. I needed to think. The sky was ablaze, Volcaryth's twin suns a painful reminder of the heat that had nearly killed *her*. I couldn't stand the thought of that happening again.

Mate.

The word echoed in my mind. This wasn't some fleeting desire. This was a bond, a connection that defied logic and tradition. My heart thrummed in my chest as I let the weight of the situation settle upon me.

A human ... How could I possibly ...

Doubt twisted around my heart, a snake trying to kill my future. What if the connection was false? What if she found me repulsive? What if she didn't want me? Despite all my rage and power, the thought made me flinch.

I was Rath Flame Heart. I commanded legions; I had faced down the greatest warriors of our time; I was the fire in our clan, yet the possibility of her rejection was more terrifying than anything. The uncertainty made me want to roar, to shake the world until reality shifted.

I pushed past the fear, the self-doubt, the uncertainty. My scales glinted as my wings snapped open, and I took to the sky, ready and determined. The ground rushed away under me as my muscles worked, propelling me upward. A plan was forming.

I needed to see her, to touch her, to mark her as mine. And nothing—especially not a stubborn old healer—would stop me.

My roar echoed through the air, a promise written in flames.

RATH'S BOOK *is coming soon!*

Thank you so much for reading *Claimed by the Drakarn Warrior Lord*!
Your support means the world to me. If you enjoyed the story, it would mean even more if you could take a moment to share your thoughts in a review or leave a rating.
Hearing from readers like you makes all the difference!

Need a little more of Terra & Darrokar?

Sign up at the link below to **receive a free bonus epilogue!**

Get your freebie!
https://katerudolph.net/index.php/darrokar-bonus/

Prince Crux is in a bind.

When the Dragon King commands Crux find a mate, his days of carefree bachelorhood are over. One trip to a psychic matchmaker and he's on the path to his destiny. But it all comes screeching to a halt when he meets a human woman who lights his inner fire and makes him yearn.

She's got a pair of roller skates and an attitude.

Courtney is supposed to be putting the shambles of her life back together. Getting abducted by aliens isn't part of the plan. Neither is getting rescued by a scorchingly hot dragon that makes her think of an impossible future. But they have no chance together if they can't first escape a planet full of monsters intent on their destruction.

Guarded by the Shifter

Werewolf. Bodyguard. Mate.
The origins of these shifters are shrouded in mystery,
but they're determined to protect their mates from
any harm that comes their way.
Also available in audio!
Hunting Season
On the Prowl
Stalking Magic
Hungry for the Wolf
Wolf Cursed (novella)
Wolf's Temptation

Stealing the Alpha

**The thief takes what she wants, but the
alpha keeps what's his…**
Join shifter thief Mel as she clashes with lion alpha
Luke in an explosive trilogy of two opposites who
can't keep away from one another.
Also available in audio!

The Alpha Heist
Entangled with the Thief
In the Alpha's Bed

Alien Mates: Planet Exile

Guerran is no place for pretty human women. But these alien heroes will protect their mates!
Also available in audio!

Exile's Hunter
Exile's Adored

Zulir Warrior Mates

Kidnapped humans. Alien Warriors. Electric wings.

The Zulir Warrior Mates series brings you human heroines and heroes abducted from Earth who find love – and wings! – with the alien warriors who rescue them.
Also available in audio!

Synnr's Saint
Synnr's Hope
Synnr's Spark
Synnr's Kiss
Synnr's Ride

Mated to the Alien

Fated Mate Alien Romance

Detyens are doomed to die young if they don't find their fated mates.

Follow along as these mated pairs fight off aliens, corrupt dictators, prejudiced humans, pirates, and more! The books can be read or listened to in any order, though some characters show up in multiple stories.

Select books available in audio.

Pick a book and jump into the action today!

Ruwen
Tyral
Stoan
Cyborg
Krayter
Kayleb

Shayn

Braxtyn

Doryan

Dekon

Detyen Warriors

Detya was destroyed a hundred years ago. These doomed warriors are out to find justice… and their mates.
The Detyen Warriors series brings you kick butt heroines, alpha alien heroes, fated mates, and relationships strong enough to span the galaxy!
The entire series is also available in audio!

Soulless

Ruthless

Heartless

Faultless

Endless

Detyen Warrior Outcasts

Fated Mate Alien Romance

These doomed warriors were abandoned by their people and live on the edge. Their mates hold the key to their salvation.

Pick a book and jump into the action today!

Dangerous Bond
Intrepid Bond
Wayward Bond

Alien Holiday Romance

Christmas... in space????

These alien holiday romances look beyond Earth's winter holidays and ring in the season across the galaxy!

Select titles available in audio.

Snowed in with the Alien Beast
The Alien's Winter Gift
The Alien Reindeer's Wild Ride
Trapped with her Alien Mate

Alien Outlaws

Outlaws, schemes, and love… it's all there in the Alien Outlaws series…

Andie Munster is sick of life on Ixilta, the planet she got dumped on after being abducted from Earth six years ago. And when the mysterious and dangerous Xandr shows up looking for a way off the planet, she's half-prisoner, half-co-conspirator in a wild rush to escape.

Rogue Alien's Escape
Rogue Alien's Woman
Rogue Alien's Secret
Rogue Alien's Legacy

Find more by Kate Rudolph at www. katerudolph.net

ABOUT KATE RUDOLPH

Kate Rudolph is a paranormal and sci-fi romance writer who lives in Indiana. She loves writing about kick butt heroines and the steamy heroes who love them. She's been devouring romance novels since she was too young to be reading them and had to hide her books so no one would take them away. She couldn't imagine a better job in this world than writing romances and sharing them with her fellow readers.

If you enjoyed this story, please consider leaving a review.